S0-AIC-734

ON
THE EDGE
OF THE
CLIFF

ON THE EDGE OF THE CLIFF

OF THE CLIFF

Short Stories by
V. S. PRITCHETT

Vintage Books • A Division of Random House • New York

First Vintage Books Edition, January 1981
Copyright © 1979 by V.S. Pritchett
All rights reserved under International and Pan-American
Copyright Conventions. Published in the United States
by Random House, Inc., New York. Originally published by Random House,
Inc., New York, in November 1979.

The author wishes to thank the editors of *The New Yorker*, *Playboy*,
The Atlantic Monthly, *The Times* (of London), *Winter's Tales*,
Woman's Journal, *Cosmopolitan* (U.K.), *Encounter* and *The New Statesman*,
in which these stories originally appeared.

"On the Edge of the Cliff" originally appeared in *The New Yorker* and
Cosmopolitan (U.K.); "A Family Man" in *The New Yorker* and *The Times*
(of London); "The Spanish Bed" in *The Atlantic Monthly* and *Woman's
Journal* (U.K.); "The Wedding" and "The Worshippers" in *Encounter*;
"The Vice-Consul" and "Tea with Mrs. Bittell" in *The New Statesman*;
"The Accompanist" in *Playboy* and *Winter's Tales* (U.K.);
and "The Fig Tree" in *The New Yorker*.

Library of Congress Cataloging in Publication Data
Pritchett, Victor Sawdon, Sir, 1900–
On the edge of the cliff.
Contents: On the edge of the cliff.—A family man.—
The Spanish bed.—The wedding. [etc.]
I. Title.
PZ3.P93950n 1981   [PR6031.R7]   823'.912   80-11970
ISBN 0-394-74047-5

Manufactured in the United States of America

For Dorothy

CONTENTS

On the Edge of the Cliff   3

A Family Man   23

The Spanish Bed   35

The Wedding   57

The Worshippers   79

The Vice-Consul   101

The Accompanist   111

Tea with Mrs. Bittell   127

The Fig Tree   151

ON THE EDGE OF THE CLIFF

The sea fog began to lift towards noon. It had been blowing in, thin and loose for two days, smudging the tops of the trees up the ravine where the house stood. "Like the cold breath of old men," Rowena wrote in an attempt at a poem, but changed the line, out of kindness, to "the breath of ghosts," because Harry might take it personally. The truth was that his breath was not foggy at all, but smelled of the dozens of cigarettes he smoked all day. He would walk about, taking little steps, with his hand outstretched, tapping the ash off as he talked. This gave an abstracted searching elegance which his heavy face and long sentences needed. In her dressing gown Rowena went to his room. His glasses were off and he had finished shaving and he turned a face savaged to the point of saintliness by age, but with a heavy underlip that made him look helplessly brutal. She laughed at the soap in his ears.

"The ghosts have gone," she said poetically. "We can go to Withy Hole! I'll drive by the Guilleth road, there's a fair there. They'll tell our fortunes."

"Dull place," he said. "It used to be full of witches in the sixteenth century."

"I'm a witch," she said. "I want to go to the fair. I saw the poster. It starts today."

"We'll go," he said, suspicious, but giving in.

He was seventyish, and with a young girl of twenty-five one had, of course, to pretend to be suspicious. There are rules for old men who are in love with young girls, all the stricter when the young girls are in love with them. It has to be played as a game.

"The sea pinks will be out on the cliffs," he said.

"You old botanist!" she said.

He was about to say "I know that" and go on to say that girls were like flowers with voices and that he had spent a lot of his life collecting both, but he had said these things to her often before and at his age one had to avoid repeating oneself, if possible. Anyway, it was more effective as a compliment when other people were there and they would turn to look at her. When young girls turned into women they lost his interest: he had always lived for reverie.

"So it's settled," she said.

Now he looked tragic as he gazed at her. Waving his razor, he began his nervous trick of taking a few dancelike steps and she gave him one of her light hugs and ran out of the room.

What with his organizing fusses and her habit of vanishing to do something to a drawing she was working on, the start was late.

"We'll have to eat something," she said, giving an order.

But it was his house, not hers. He'd lived alone long enough not to be able to stand a woman in his kitchen, could not bear to see her cut a loaf or muddle the knives and forks or choke the sink with tea leaves.

"Rowena and I," he said to people who came to see them, in his military voice, "eat very little. We see no one."

This was not true, but like a general with a literary turn, he organized his imagination. He was much guided by literature. His wife had gone mad and had killed herself. So in the house he saw himself as a Mr. Rochester, or in the car as Count Mosca with the young duchess in *La Chartreuse de Parme;* if they met people, as Tolstoy's worldly Aunt. This was another game: it educated the girl.

While he fussed between the kitchen and the room they ate in, she came down late and idled, throwing back her long black hair, lassoing him with smiles and side glances thrown out and rushed at him while he had a butter plate in his hand and gave him another of her light engulfing hugs and laughed at the plate he waved in the air.

"Rowena!" he shouted, for she had gone off again. "Get the car out."

The house was halfway up the long ravine, backed and faced by an army of ash trees and beeches. There was the terrace and the ingenious steep garden and the plants that occupied him most of the day, and down from the terrace he had to cut the twenty or thirty steps himself, heaving his pickaxe. Rowena had watched his thick stack of coarse grey hair and his really rather brutal face and his pushed-out lips, as he hacked and the pick hit the stones. He worked with such anger and pride; but he looked up at her sometimes with appealing, brilliant eyes. His furious ancient's face contained pain naturally.

She knew he hated to be told to be careful when he came down the steps. She knew the ceremony of getting him into the car, for he was a tall angular man and had to fold himself in, his knees nearly touching his chin, to which the long deep despondent lines of his face ran heavily down. It was exciting for her to drive the old man dangerously fast down the long circling lane through the trees, to show how dangerous she could be, while he talked. He would talk nonstop for the next hour, beginning, of course, with the country fair.

"It's no good. Plastic, like cheap food. Not worth seeing. The twentieth century has packaged everything."

And he was on to the pre-Roman times, the ancient spirit of carnival, Celtic gods and devils, as they drove out of the ravine into deep lanes, where he could name the ferns in the stone walls, and the twisting hills and corners that shook the teeth and the spine. Historical instances poured out of him. He was, she said, Old Father Time himself, but he did not take that as a joke, though he humored her with a small laugh. It was part of the game. He was not Father Time, for in one's seventies, one is a miser of time, putting it by, hiding the minutes, while she spent fast, not knowing she was living in time at all.

Guilleth was a dull, dusty, Methodistical little town with geraniums in the windows of the houses. Sammy's Fair was in a rough field just outside it, where dogs and children ran about. There was only one shooting gallery; they were still putting up the back canvas of the coconut shy. There were hoopla stalls, a lot of shouting and few customers. But the small roundabout gave out its engine whistle and the children packed the vulgar circle of spotted cows with huge pink udders, the rocking horses, the pigs, the tigers and a pair of giraffes.

The professor regarded it as a cultural pathos. He feared Rowena. She was quite childishly cruel to him. With a beautiful arrogance that mocked him, she got out of the car and headed for ice cream. He had to head her off the goldfish in their bowls. She'd probably want to bring one home.

"Give me some money," she said, going to the roundabout. There was a small crowd near that. "I'm going on the giraffe. Come on."

"I'll watch you," he complained and cleaned his glasses.

There she was, riding a giraffe already, tall and like a schoolmistress among the town children, with her long hair, which she kept on throwing back as she whirled round, a young miracle, getting younger and younger. There were other girls. There were town youths and there was an idiotic young man riding backwards on a cow, kicking out his legs and every now and then waving to the crowd. Rowena on her giraffe did not smile, but as she came round sedately, waved to the old man as she sailed by.

He looked at his watch. How much longer?

"I'm going on again," she called, and did not get off.

He found himself absurdly among the other patient watchers, older than all, better dressed too, on his dignity, all curiosity gone. He moved away to separate himself from his bunch of them, but he had the impression they all moved with him. There was a young woman in a bright-red coat who always seemed to be in the next bunch he joined. Round came the giraffe: round came the young man on the cow. The young woman in red waved. Seeing that to wave was the correct thing, the old man too waved at the giraffe. The woman waved again a moment later and stared at him as if annoyed. He moved a yard from her, then five yards, then to the other side of the roundabout. Here he could wave without being conspicuous, yet the woman was standing close to him once more. She was small with reddish hair, her chin up, looking at him.

"You don't remember me," she accused him in a high voice. Her small eyes were impudent. He stepped back, gaping.

"Daisy Pyke," she said.

Pyke? Pyke? He gaped at her briefly, his mind was sailing round with Rowena.

"George's wife," she said, challenging his stupidity.

"George . . ." But he stopped. George Pyke's wife must be fifty by now. This woman could not be more than thirty. Her daughter —had they had a daughter?

"Have I changed as much as that?" she said. Her manner was urchinlike and she grinned with pleasure at his confusion and then her mouth drooped at the corners plaintively, begging. Nowadays he thought only of Rowena's wide mouth, which made all other women vague to him. And then the hard little begging, pushing mouth and its high voice broke into his memory. He stepped back with embarrassment and a short stare of horror which he covered quickly, his feet dancing a few steps, and saying with foolish smiles, "Daisy! I thought . . . I was watching that thing. What are you doing here?"

Now that he remembered, he could not conceal a note of indignation and he stood still, his eyes peered coldly. He could see this had its effect on her.

"The same as you," she said in that curt offhand voice. "Waiting. Waiting for them to come off." And she turned away from him, offended, waved wildly at the roundabout and shouted, "Stephen, you fool!" The young man riding backwards on the cow waved back and shouted to her.

What an appalling thing! But there it is—one must expect it when one is old: the map in one's head, indeed the literal map of the country empties and loses its contours, towns and villages, and people sink out of sight. The protective faces of friends vanish and one is suddenly alone, naked and exposed. The population ranked between oneself and old enemies suddenly dissolves and the enemy stands before one. Daisy Pyke!

The old man could not get away. He said as politely as he could manage, "I thought you went abroad. How is George?"

"We did. George," she said, "died in Spain." And added briskly, "On a golf course."

"I'm sorry. I didn't know."

She looked back at the roundabout and turned again to say to him, "I know all about *you*. You've got a new house at Colfe. I've still got the old house, though actually it's let."

Forty miles lay between Colfe and Daisy Pyke—but no people in between! Now the roundabout stopped. There was a scramble of children getting on and getting off, and the local watchers moved forward too.

"I must get Rowena," he said ruthlessly and he hurried off, calling out in his peremptory voice, "Rowena!"

He knew that Daisy Pyke was watching him as he held out a hand to help Rowena off, but Rowena ignored it and jumped off herself.

"Rowena. We must go."

"Why? It was lovely. Did you see that ridiculous young man?"

"No, Rowena," he said. "Where?"

"Over there," she said, "with the girl in red, the one you were chatting up, you old rip. I saw you!" She laughed and took his arm. "You're blushing."

"She's not a girl," he said. "She's a woman I used to know in London twenty years ago. It was rather awful! I didn't recognize her. I used to know her husband. She used to be a friend of Violet's."

"Violet's!" said Rowena. "But you *must* introduce me." She was always eager to know, as if to possess, everyone he had ever known, to have all of him, even the dead. Above all Violet, his wife. Rowena longed to be as old as that dead woman.

"Really, Harry, you are frightful with people."

"Oh well . . . But she's appalling. We had a terrible row."

"One of your old loves," she teased.

"I had to throw her out of the house," he said. "She's a liar."

"Then I *must* see her," said Rowena. "How thrilling."

"I think they've gone," he said.

"No," said Rowena. "There they are. Take me over."

And she pulled him towards the hoopla stall where Daisy Pyke and the young man were standing. There lay the delightfulness of Rowena: she freed him from the boredom into which his memories had set and hardened. He had known many young girls who, in this situation, would be eagerly storing opportunities for jealousy of his past life. Rowena was not like that.

At the stall, with its cunningly arranged bowls, jugs and toys, the young man with the yellow curling hair was pitching rings onto the table, telling Daisy to try and altering the angle of the ring in her hand.

"Choose what you want, hold the ring level and lightly, don't skim fast. Don't bowl it like that! Like this."

Daisy's boldness had gone. She was fond and serious, glancing at the young man before she threw.

"Daisy," said the old man, putting on a shady and formal manner as if he were at a party, "I have brought Rowena to meet you."

And Rowena stepped forward gushingly. "How d'you do! I was telling Harry about the young man on the cow."

"Here he is," said Daisy stiffly. "Stephen!"

The young man turned and said "Hello" and went on throwing rings. "Like that," he said.

Rowena watched him mockingly.

"We are just off," said Harry.

"I've heard a lot about you," said Daisy to Rowena.

"We're going to walk along the cliffs," said Harry.

"To Withy Hole," said Rowena.

"It was extraordinary meeting you here," said Harry.

"Perhaps," said Daisy, "we'll meet again."

"Oh well—you know we hardly see anyone now," said Harry.

Daisy studied Rowena impudently and she laughed at the boy, who had failed again.

"I won a goldfish once," said Rowena, laughing. "It died on the way home."

"Extraordinary," the old man said as he and Rowena walked away. "That must be George's son, but taller. George was short."

When she got him back into the car she saw by his leaden look that the subject was closed. She had met one more of his friends— that was the main thing.

The hills seemed to pile up and the sea to get farther and farther away and then, suddenly, as they got over the last long hill, passing the caravan sites that were empty at this time of the year and looked like those flat white Andalusian towns he remembered, from a distance. The old man was saying, "But we have this new rootless civilization, anarchic but standardized"—suddenly the sea appeared between the dunes below, not grey and choppy, but deep-blue, all candor, like a young mouth, between the dunes and beyond it, wide and still and sleepily serene. The old man was suddenly in command, fussing about the exact place where they could leave the car, struggling over the sand dunes dotted with last year's litter, on to the huge cliffs. At the top there they could look back and see on the wide bay the shallow sea breaking idly, in changing lines of surf, like lips speaking lines that broke unfinished and could not be heard. A long way off a dozen surfers were wading out, deeper and deeper, towards the bigger waves as if they were leaving the land for good and might be trying to reach the horizon. Rowena stopped to gaze at them, waiting for one of them to come in on a long glissade, but the old

man urged her on to the close turf of the cliffs. That is what he had
come for: boundlessness, distance. For thirty miles on a clear day in
May like this, one could walk without meeting a soul, from headland
to headland, gazing through the hum of the wind and under the cries
of the dashing gulls, at what seemed to be an unending procession
of fading promontories, each dropping to its sandy cove, yet still
riding out into the water. The wind did not move the old man's
tough thatch of hair but made his big ears stick out. Rowena bound
her loose hair with a scarf. From low cliff to high cliff, over the
cropped turf, which was like a carpet, where the millions of sea pinks
and daisies were scattered, mile after mile in their colonies, the old
man led the way, digging his knees into the air, gesticulating, talking,
pointing to a kestrel above or a cormorant black as soot on a rock,
while she followed lazily yards behind him. He stopped impatiently
to show her some small cushioned plant or stood on the cliff's edge,
like a prophet, pointing down to the falls of rock, the canyons,
caverns and the tunnels into which the green water poured in black
and was sucked out into green again and spilled in waterfalls down
the outer rocks. The old man was a strong walker, bending to it, but
when he stopped he straightened and Rowena smiled at his air of
detachment as he gazed at distant things as if he knew them. To her
he looked like a frightening mixture of pagan saint and toiling
animal. They would rest at the crest of a black cliff for a few minutes,
feel the sun burn their skin and then on they went.

"We can't see the bay any more," she said. She was thinking of
the surfriders.

"The cliff after the next is the Hole," he said and pulled her to
her feet.

"Yes, the Hole," she said.

He had a kind of mania about the Hole. This was the walk he liked
best and so did she, except for that ugly final horror. The sea had
tunnelled under the rock in several places along this wild coast and
had sucked out enormous slaty craters fifty yards across and this one
a hundred and eighty feet deep, so that even at the edge one could
not see the water pouring in. One stood listening for the bump of
hidden water on a quiet day: on wild ones it seethed in the bottom
of the pot. The place terrified Rowena and she held back, but he

stumbled through the rough grasses to the edge, calling back bits of geology and navigation—and to amuse her, explained how smugglers had had to wait for the low wave to take them in.

Now, once more, they were looking at the great meaningless wound. As he stood at the edge he seemed to her to be at one with it. It reminded her of his mouth when she had once seen it (with a horror she tried to wipe from her mind) before he had put his dentures in. Of her father's too.

Well, the objective was achieved. They found a bank on the seaward side out of the wind where the sun burned and they rested.

"Heaven," she said and closed her eyes.

They sat in silence for a long time but he gazed at the rising floor of eventless water. Far out, from time to time, in some small eddy of the wind, little families of whitecaps would appear. They were like faces popping up or perhaps white hands shooting out and disappearing pointlessly. Yes, they were the pointless dead.

"What are you thinking about?" she asked without opening her eyes.

He was going to say "At my age one is always thinking about death," but he said "You."

"What about me?" she said with that shamelessness of girls.

"Your ears," he said.

"You are a liar," she said. "You're thinking about Daisy Pyke."

"Not now," he said.

"But you must be," she said. She pointed. "Isn't the cove just below where you all used to bathe with nothing on? Did she come?"

"Round the corner," he said, correcting her. "Violet and I used to bathe there. Everyone came. Daisy came once when George was on the golf course. She swam up and down, hour after hour, as cold as a fish. Hopeless on dry land. Gordon and Vera came, but Daisy only once. She didn't fit in—very conventional—sat telling dirty stories. Then she went swimming, to clean up. George was playing golf all day and bridge all evening; that didn't go down well. They had a dartboard in their house: the target was a naked woman. A pretty awful, jokey couple. You can guess the bull's-eye."

"What was this row?" she said.

"She told lies," he said, turning to her. And he said this with a hiss of finality which she knew. She waited for one of his stories, but it did not come.

"I want to swim in the cove," said Rowena.

"It's too cold this time of the year," he said.

"I want to go," she said.

"It's a long way down and hard coming back."

"Yes, but I want to go—where you all used to go."

She was obstinate about this and, of course, he liked that.

"All right," he said, getting up. Like all girls she wanted to leave her mark on places. He noticed how she was impelled to touch pictures in galleries when he had taken her to Italy. Ownership! Power! He used to dislike that but now he did not; the change was a symptom of his adoration of her. And she did want to go. She did want to assert her presence on that empty sand, to make the sand feel her mark.

They scrambled the long way down the rocks until the torn cliffs were gigantic above them. On the smooth sand she ran barefoot to the edge of the sea rippling in.

"It's ice!" she screamed.

He stood there, hunched. There was a litter of last year's rags and cartons near the rocks. Summer crowds now swarmed into the place, which had been secret. He glowered with anger at the debris.

"I'm going to pee," he said.

She watched the sea, for he was a long time gone.

"That was a big one," she shouted.

But he was not there. He was out on the rocks, he had pulled off his clothes. He was standing there, his body furred with grey hair, his belly wrinkled, his thighs shrunk. Up went his bony arms.

"You're not to! It will kill you! Your heart!" she shouted.

He gave a wicked laugh, she saw his yellow teeth, and in he dived and was crawling and shouting in the water as he swam out farther, defying her, threshing the water, and then as she screamed at him, really frightened, he came crawling in like some ugly hairy sea animal, his skin reddened with cold, and stood dripping with his arms wide as if he was going to give a howl. He climbed over the rocks and back to the sand and got his clothes and was drying himself with his shirt.

"You're mad," she said. "You're not to put that wet thing on."

"It will dry in this sun," he said.

"What was all that for?" she said. "Did you find her?"

"Who?" he said, looking round in bewilderment. He had dived in boastfully and in a kind of rage, a rage against time, a rage against Daisy Pyke too. He did not answer, but looked at her with a glint of shrewdness in his eyes. She was flattered by the glitter in this look from a sometimes terrifying old man.

He was tired now and they took the short inland road to the car close to those awful caravans, and when she got him into the car again he fell asleep and snorted. He went to his room early but could not sleep; he had broken one of his rules for old men. For the first time he had let her see him naked. He was astounded when she came into his room and got into his bed: she had not done this before. "I've come to see the Ancient Mariner," she said.

How marvelous. She is jealous, after all. She loves me, he went about saying to himself in the next weeks. She drove to what they called "our town" to buy cakes. "I am so thin," she said.

The first time she returned saying she had seen his "dear friend Daisy." She was in the supermarket.

"What's she doing there?" he said. "She lives forty miles away. What did she say?"

"We did not speak. I mean, I don't think she saw me. Her son was with her. He said hello. He'd got the hood of the car up. She came out and gave me a nod—I don't think she likes me," she said with satisfaction.

The next week she went again to get petrol. The old man stayed at the house, shook one or two mats and swept the sitting-room floor. It was his house and Rowena was untidy. Then he sat on the terrace, listening for her car, anxiously.

Presently he picked up the sound, much earlier than her usual time, and saw the distant glint in the trees as the car wound its way up. There she was, threading her beauty through the trees. He heard with alarm the sudden silences of the car at some turn in the hill, then heard it getting louder as it turned a corner, then passing into silence again. He put his book down and went inside in a dutiful panic to put the kettle on, and while he waited for it to boil he took the cups out pedantically, one by one, to the table on the terrace and stood listening again. Now it was on the last stretch, now he heard a crackling of wheels below. He ran in to heat the teapot and ran out with his usual phrase: "Did you get what you wanted?"

Then, puffing up the last steps, she came. But it was not she; it was a small woman, bare-legged and in sandals, with a swaggering urchin grin on her face, pulling a scarf off her head. Daisy!

"Gosh!" she said.

Harry skipped back a yard and stood, straightening and forbidding. "Daisy!" he said, annoyed, as if waving her off.

"Those steps! Harry!" she said. "Gosh, what a view."

She gave a dry dismissive laugh at it. She had, he remembered, always defied what she saw. The day when he had seen her at the fair seemed to slide away under his feet and years slid by, after that, following that day.

"What—" he began. Then in his military way, he jerked out, "Rowena's gone into town. I am waiting for her."

"I know," said Daisy. "Can I sit down and get my breath? I know. I saw her." And with a plotting satisfaction: "Not to speak to. She passed me. Ah, that's better."

"We never see people," said Harry sternly. "You see I am working. If the telephone rings, we don't answer it."

"The same with us. I hope I'm not interrupting. I thought—I'll dash up, just for a minute."

"And Rowena has her work . . ." he said. Daisy was always an interrupter.

"I gave you a surprise," said Daisy comfortably. "She is lovely. That's why I came. You're lucky—how d'you do it? Where did you find her? And what a place you've got here! I made Stephen go and see his friends. It was such a long time—years, isn't it? I had to come. You haven't changed, you know. But you didn't recognize me, did you? You were trying not to see me, weren't you?"

Her eyes and her nose were small. She is at her old game of shock tactics, he thought. He looked blankly at her.

"I explained that," he said nervously. "I must go and turn the kettle off," he said. He paused to listen for Rowena's car, but there was no sound.

"Well," she said. "There you are. Time goes on."

When he came back with a teapot and another cup, she said, "I knew you wouldn't come and see me, so I came to see you. Let me see," she said and took off the scarf from her head. "I told you George died, didn't I? Of course I did," she said briskly.

"Yes."

"Well . . ." she said. "Harry, I had to see you. You are the only wise man I know." She looked nervously at the garden and across to the army of trees stacked on the hill and then turned to him. "You're happy and I am happy, Harry. I didn't come to make a scene and drag it all up. I was in love with you, that was the trouble, but I'm not now. I was wrong about you, about you and Violet. I couldn't bear to see her suffer. I was out of my mind. I couldn't bear to see you grieving for her. I soon knew what it was when poor George died. Harry, I just don't want you to hate me any more. I mean, you're not still furious, are you? We do change. The past is past."

The little liar, he thought. What has she come up here for? To cause trouble between himself and Rowena as she had tried to do with his wife and himself. He remembered Daisy's favorite word: honesty. She was trying for some reason to confuse him about things he had settled a long time ago in his mind.

He changed the subject. "What is—"—he frowned—"I'm sorry I can't remember names nowadays—your son doing?"

She was quick to notice the change, he saw. Nothing ever escaped Daisy.

"Oh, Tommy, the ridiculous Tommy. He's in Africa," she said, merrily dismissing him. "Well, it was better for him—problems. I'm a problem to him—George was so jealous too."

"He looks exactly like George," Harry said. "Taller, of course, the curly hair."

"What are you talking about? You haven't seen him since he was four." She laughed.

"Don't be stupid, Daisy, we saw him last week at that—what is the name of the place?—at the fair."

The blood went from Daisy's face. She raised her chin. "That's a nasty one," she said and gave her head a fierce shake. "You meant it to, didn't you? That was Stephen. I thought you'd be the last to think a thing like that, with your Rowena. I expect people say it and I don't care and if anyone said it to him he wouldn't know what they were talking about. Stephen's my lover."

The old sentimental wheedling Daisy was in the coy smile that quickly followed her sharpness. "He's mad about me," she said. "I may be old enough to be his mother, but he's sick of squealing, sulky girls of seventeen. If we had met years ago, he would have hated me. Seriously, Harry, I'd go down on my knees to him."

"I am sorry—I—that's why I didn't recognize you. You can ask Rowena. I said to her, 'That's Daisy Pyke's daughter,' " Harry said, "when I saw you."

Daisy gaped at him and slowly her lips curled up with delight. "Oh good! Is that true? Is it? You always told the truth. You really thought that! Thank you, Harry, that's the nicest thing you ever said to me. I love you for it."

She leaned forward, appealing to him quietly.

"George never slept with me for seven years before he died. Don't ask me about it, but that's the truth. I'd forgotten what it was. When Stephen asked me I thought it was an insult—you know, all this rape about. I got into the car and slammed the door in his face and left him on the road—well, not on the road, but wherever it was—and drove off. I looked back. He was still standing there. Well, I mean, at my age! That next day—*you* know what it is with women better than anyone—I was in such a mood. When I got back to the house I shouted for George, howled for him to come back and poured myself a tumblerful of whisky and wandered about the house slopping it on the carpet." She laughed. "George would have killed me for *that* if he had come—and I went out into the garden and there was Stephen, you won't believe it, walking bold as brass up from the gate. He came up quickly and just took the glass from me very politely—the stuff was pouring down my dress—and put it on the grass and he wiped my blouse. That's what did it."

She paused thoughtfully and frowned. "Not there," she said prudishly, "not at the house, of course. I wanted to get away from it. I can't bear it. We went to the caravan camp. That's where he was living. I don't know why I'm telling you this. I mean, there's a lot more."

She paused. "Love is something at our age, isn't it? I mean, when I saw you and Rowena at Guilleth—I thought I must go and talk to you. Being in the same boat."

"We're not," he said, annoyed. "I am twenty years older than you."

"Thirty, if you don't mind," she said, opening her bag and looking into her mirror. When she had put it away with a snap she looked over the flowers in the steep garden to the woods. She was listening for the sound of a car. He realized he had stopped listening for it. He found himself enjoying this hour, despite his suspicions of her. It drove away the terrors that seemed to dissolve even the trees of the ravine. With women, nature returned to its place, the trees became real trees. One lived in a long moment in which time had stopped. He did not care for Daisy, but she had that power of enticement which lay in stirring one with the illusion that she was defying one to put her right. With Rowena he had thrown away his vanity; with Daisy it returned.

"Where did you and Rowena go the day we saw you?" she asked suddenly.

"Along the cliffs," he said.

"You didn't go to the cove, did you? It's a long way. And you can't swim at this time of the year."

"We went to the cove and I *did* swim," he said. "I wouldn't let Rowena."

"I should hope not! You don't forget old times, do you?" She laughed coolly. "I hope you didn't tell Rowena—young girls can be so jealous. I *was*—d'you remember? Gosh, I'm glad I'm not young still, aren't you?"

"Stop being so romantic, Daisy," said the old man.

"Oh, I'm not romantic any more," she said. "It doesn't pay else one would pity *them*, Rowena and Stephen. So you did go to the cove—did you think of me?"

"I only think of death now," he said.

"You always were an interesting man, the type that goes on to his

nineties, like they do now," she said. "I never think about it. Stephen
would have a fit. He doesn't even know what he's going to *do*. Last
week he thought he'd be a beach guard. Or teach tennis. Or a singer!
He was surfing on the beach when I first saw him. He was living at
the camp."

She paused, offended. "Did you know they switch off the electric
light at ten o'clock at the office in those places? No one protests. Like
sheep. It would make me furious to be treated like that. You could
hear everyone snoring at once. Not that we joined in, I must say.
Actually, we're staying in his mother's house now, the bunks are too
narrow in those caravans, but she's come back. So we're looking for
something—I've let my house. The money is useful."

The old man was alarmed. He was still trying to make out the real
reason for her visit. He remembered the old Daisy—there was always
a hidden motive, something she was trying out. And he started
listening urgently again for Rowena's car. I know what it is, he
thought; she wants to move in here!

"I'm afraid it would be impossible to have you here," he said.

"Here, Harry?" she said astonished. "None of that! That's not
what I came for. Anyway," she said archly, "I wouldn't trust you."

But she considered the windows and the doors of the house and
then the view. She gave a businesslike sniff and said seriously, "You
can't keep her a prisoner here. It won't last."

"Rowena is not a prisoner. She can come and go when she likes.
We understand that."

"It depends what you mean by coming and going," said Daisy
shrewdly. "You mean *you* are the prisoner. That is it! So am I!"

"Oh," said Harry. "Love is always like that. I live only for her."

"That is it! I will tell you why I came to see you, Harry. When
I saw Rowena in town I kept out of her way. You won't believe it
—I can be tactful."

She became very serious. "Because I don't want us to meet again."
It was an open declaration. "I mean not see you for a long time, I
mean all of us. You see, Rowena is so beautiful and Stephen—well,
you've seen him. You and I would start talking about old times and
people, and they'd be left out and drawn together—now, wouldn't

they? I just couldn't bear to see him talking to her, looking at her. I wish we had not met down at the fair. It's all right now, he's with his surfing friends, but you understand?"

She got up and said, "I mean it, Harry. I know what would happen and so do you and I don't want to *see* it happen."

She went up to him because he had stood up and she tapped him hard on the chest with her firm bold finger. He could feel it on his skin, a determined blow, after she had stepped away.

"I know it can't last," she said. "And you know it can't. But I don't want *you* to see it happen," she said in her old hard taunting style. "We never really use your town anyway. I'll see *he* doesn't. Give me your word. We've got to do this for each other. We've managed quite well all these years, haven't we? And it's not saying we'll *never* meet someday, is it?"

"You're a bitch, Daisy," he said and he smiled.

"Yes, I'm a bitch still, Harry," she said. "But I'm not a fool."

She put out her hand again and he feared she was going to dig that hard finger in his chest again, but she didn't. She tied her scarf round her hair. "If anything happened I'd throw myself down Withy Hole."

"Stop being so melodramatic, Daisy," he said.

"Well, I don't want you conniving," she said coarsely. "I don't want any of your little arrangements."

And she turned to the ravine and listened. "Car coming up," she said.

"Rowena," he said.

"I'll be off. Remember."

"Be careful at the turns," he said helplessly. "She drives fast. You'll pass her on the road."

They did not kiss or even shake hands. He listened to her cursing the steps as she went down and calling out, "I bet you dug out these bloody steps yourself."

He listened to the two cars whining their way towards each other as they circled below, now Rowena's car glinted, now Daisy's. At last Rowena's slowed down at the steps, spitting stones.

Rowena came up and said, "I've just passed Daisy on the road."

"Yes, she's been here. What a tale!"

She looked at the empty cups. "And you didn't give your dearest friend any tea, you wretch."

"Oh, tea—no—er—she didn't want any," he stammered.

"As gripping as all that, was it?" she laughed.

"Very," he said. "She's talking of marrying that young man. Stephen's not her son."

"You can't mean that," she said, putting on a very proper air. "She's old enough—" but she stopped, and instead of giving him one of her light hugs, she rumpled his hair. "People do confide in you, I must say," she said. "I don't think I like her coming up here. Tell me what she said."

A
FAMILY
MAN

L ate in the afternoon, when she had given him up and had even changed out of her pink dress into her smock and jeans and was working once more at her bench, the doorbell rang. William had come, after all. It was in the nature of their love affair that his visits were fitful: he had a wife and children. To show that she understood the situation, even found the curious satisfaction of reverie in his absences that lately had lasted several weeks, Berenice dawdled yawning to the door. As she slipped off the chain, she called back into the empty flat, "It's all right, Father. I'll answer it."

William had told her to do this because she was a woman living on her own: the call would show strangers that there was a man there to defend her. Berenice's voice was mocking, for she thought his idea possessive and ridiculous; not only that, she had been brought up by Quakers and thought it wrong to tell or act a lie. Sometimes, when she opened the door to him, she would say, "Well! Mr. Cork," to remind him he was a married man. He had the kind of shadowed handsomeness that easily gleams with guilt, and for her this gave their affair its piquancy.

But now—when she opened the door—no William, and the yawn, its hopes and its irony, died on her mouth. A very large woman, taller than herself, filled the doorway from top to bottom, an enormous blob of pink jersey and green skirt, the jersey low and loose at the neck, a face and body inflated to the point of speechlessness. She even seemed to be asleep with her large blue eyes open.

"Yes?" said Berenice.

The woman woke up and looked unbelievingly at Berenice's feet, which were bare, for she liked to go about barefoot at home, and said, "Is this Miss Foster's place?"

Berenice was offended by the word "place." "This is Miss Foster's residence. I am she."

"Ah," said the woman, babyish no longer but sugary. "I was given your address at the College. You teach at the College, I believe? I've come about the repair."

"A repair? I make jewelry," said Berenice. "I do not do repairs."

"They told me at the College you were repairing my husband's flute. I am Mrs. Cork."

Berenice's heart stopped. Her wrist went weak and her hand drooped on the door handle, and a spurt of icy air shot up her body to her face and then turned to boiling heat as it shot back again. Her head suddenly filled with chattering voices saying, Oh God. How frightful! William, you didn't tell her? Now, what are you, you, you going to do. And the word "Do, do" clattered on in her head.

"Cork?" said Berenice. "Flute?"

"Florence Cork," said the woman firmly, all sleepy sweetness gone.

"Oh yes. I am sorry. Mrs. Cork. Of course, yes. Oh, do come in. I'm so sorry. We haven't met, how very nice to meet you. William's —Mr. Cork's—flute! His flute. Yes, I remember. How d'you do? How is he? He hasn't been to the College for months. Have you seen him lately—how silly, of course you have. Did you have a lovely holiday? Did the children enjoy it? I would have posted it, only I didn't know your address. Come in, please, come in."

"In here?" said Mrs. Cork and marched into the front room where Berenice worked. Here, in the direct glare of Berenice's working lamp, Florence Cork looked even larger and even pregnant. She seemed to occupy the whole of the room as she stood in it, memorizing everything—the bench, the pots of paintbrushes, the large designs pinned to the wall, the rolls of paper, the sofa covered with papers and letters and sewing, the pink dress which Berenice had thrown over a chair. She seemed to be consuming it all, drinking all the air.

But here, in the disorder of which she was very vain, which indeed fascinated her, and represented her talent, her independence, a girl's right to a life of her own and, above all, being barefooted, helped Berenice recover her breath.

"It is such a pleasure to meet you. Mr. Cork has often spoken of you to us at the College. We're quite a family there. Please sit. I'll move the dress. I was mending it."

But Mrs. Cork did not sit down. She gave a sudden lurch towards the bench, and seeing her husband's flute there propped against the wall, she grabbed it and swung it above her head as if it were a weapon.

"Yes," said Berenice, who was thinking, Oh dear, the woman's drunk, "I was working on it only this morning. I had never seen a flute like that before. Such a beautiful silver scroll. I gather it's very old, a German one, a presentation piece given to Mr. Cork's father. I believe he played in a famous orchestra—where was it?—Bayreuth or Berlin? You never see a scroll like that in England, not a delicate silver scroll like that. It seems to have been dropped somewhere or have had a blow. Mr. Cork told me he had played it in an orchestra himself once, Covent Garden or somewhere . . ."

She watched Mrs. Cork flourish the flute in the air.

"A blow," cried Mrs. Cork now in a rich voice. "I'll say it did. I threw it at him."

And then she lowered her arm and stood swaying on her legs as she confronted Berenice and said, "Where is he?"

"Who?" said Berenice in a fright.

"My husband!" Mrs. Cork shouted. "Don't try and soft-soap me with all that twaddle. Playing in an orchestra! Is that what he has been stuffing you up with? I know what you and he are up to. He comes every Thursday. He's been here since half past two. I know. I have had this place watched."

She swung round to the closed door of Berenice's bedroom. "What's in there?" she shouted and advanced to it.

"Mrs. Cork," said Berenice as calmly as she could. "Please stop shouting. I know nothing about your husband. I don't know what you are talking about." And she placed herself before the door of the room. "And please stop shouting. That is my father's room." And, excited by Mrs. Cork's accusation, she said, "He is a very old man and he is not well. He is asleep in there."

"In there?" said Mrs. Cork.

"Yes, in there."

"And what about the other rooms? Who lives upstairs?"

"There are no other rooms," said Berenice. "I live here with my father. Upstairs? Some new people have moved in."

Berenice was astonished by these words of hers, for she was a truthful young woman and was astonished, even excited, by a lie so vast. It seemed to glitter in the air as she spoke it.

Mrs. Cork was checked. She flopped down on the chair on which Berenice had put her dress.

"My dress, if you please," said Berenice and pulled it away.

"If you don't do it here," said Mrs. Cork, quietening and with tears in her eyes, "you do it somewhere else."

"I don't know anything about your husband. I only see him at the College like the other teachers. I don't know anything about him. If you will give me the flute, I will pack it up for you and I must ask you to go."

"You can't deceive me. I know everything. You think because you are young you can do what you like," Mrs. Cork muttered to herself and began rummaging in her handbag.

For Berenice one of the attractions of William was that their meetings were erratic. The affair was like a game: she liked surprise above all. In the intervals when he was not there, the game continued for her. She liked imagining what he and his family were doing. She saw them as all glued together as if in some enduring and absurd photograph, perhaps sitting in their suburban garden, or standing beside a motorcar, always in the sun, but William himself, dark-faced and busy in his gravity, a step or two back from them.

"Is your wife beautiful?" she asked him once when they were in bed.

William in his slow serious way took a long time to answer. He said at last, "Very beautiful."

This had made Berenice feel exceedingly beautiful herself. She saw his wife as a raven-haired, dark-eyed woman and longed to meet her. The more she imagined her, the more she felt for her, the more she saw eye to eye with her in the pleasant busy middle ground of womanish feelings and moods, for as a woman living alone she felt a firm loyalty to her sex. During this last summer when the family were on holiday she had seen them glued together again as they sat with dozens of other families in the airplane that was taking them abroad, so that it seemed to her that the London sky was rumbling day after day, night after night, with matrimony 30,000 feet above the city, the countryside, the sea and its beaches where she imagined the legs of their children running across the sand, William flushed with his responsibilities, wife turning over to brown her back in the sun. Berenice was often out and about with her many friends, most of whom were married. She loved the look of harassed contentment, even the tired faces of the husbands, the alert looks of their spirited wives. Among the married she felt her singularity. She listened to their endearments and to their bickerings. She played with their children, who ran at once to her. She could not bear the young men who approached her, talking about themselves all the time, flashing with the slapdash egotisms of young men trying to bring her peculiarity to an end. Among families she felt herself to be strange and necessary—a necessary secret. When William had said his wife was beautiful, she felt so beautiful herself that her bones seemed to turn to water.

But now the real Florence sat rummaging in her bag before her, this balloonlike giant, first babyish and then shouting accusations, the dreamed-of Florence vanished. This real Florence seemed unreal and incredible. And William himself changed. His good looks began to look commonplace and shady: his seriousness became furtive, his praise of her calculating. He was shorter than his wife, his face now looked hangdog and she saw him dragging his feet as obediently he followed her. She resented that this woman had made her tell a lie, strangely intoxicating though it was to do so, and had made her feel as ugly as his wife was. For she must be, if Florence was what he called "beautiful." And not only ugly, but pathetic and without dignity.

Berenice watched warily as the woman took a letter from her handbag.

"Then what is this necklace?" she said, blowing herself out again.

"What necklace is this?" said Berenice.

"Read it. You wrote it."

Berenice smiled with astonishment: she knew she needed no longer to defend herself. She prided herself on fastidiousness: she had never in her life written a letter to a lover—it would be like giving something of herself away, it would be almost an indecency. She certainly felt it to be very wrong to read anyone else's letters, as Mrs. Cork pushed the letter at her. Berenice took it in two fingers, glanced and turned it over to see the name of the writer.

"This is not my writing," she said. The hand was sprawling; her own was scratchy and small. "Who is Bunny? Who is Rosie?"

Mrs. Cork snatched the letter and read in a booming voice that made the words ridiculous: " 'I am longing for the necklace. Tell that girl to hurry up. Do bring it next time. And darling, don't forget the flute!!! Rosie.' What do you mean, who is Bunny?" Mrs. Cork said. "You know very well. Bunny is my husband."

Berenice turned away and pointed to a small poster that was pinned to the wall. It contained a photograph of a necklace and three brooches she had shown at an exhibition in a very fashionable shop known for selling modern jewelry. At the bottom of the poster, elegantly printed, were the words

Created by Berenice

Berenice read the words aloud, reciting them as if they were a line from a poem: "My name is Berenice," she said.

It was strange to be speaking the truth. And it suddenly seemed to her, as she recited the words, that really William had never been to her flat, that he had never been her lover, and had never played his silly flute there, that indeed he was the most boring man at the College and that a chasm separated her from this woman, whom jealousy had made so ugly.

Mrs. Cork was still swelling with unbelief, but as she studied the poster, despair settled on her face. "I found it in his pocket," she said helplessly.

"We all make mistakes, Mrs. Cork," Berenice said coldly across the chasm. And then, to be generous in victory, she said, "Let me see the letter again."

Mrs. Cork gave her the letter and Berenice read it and at the word "flute" a doubt came into her head. Her hand began to tremble and quickly she gave the letter back. "Who gave you my address—I mean, at the College?" Berenice accused. "There is a rule that no addresses are given. Or telephone numbers."

"The girl," said Mrs. Cork, defending herself.

"Which girl? At Inquiries?"

"She fetched someone."

"Who was it?" said Berenice.

"I don't know. It began with a *W*, I think," said Mrs. Cork.

"Wheeler?" said Berenice. "There is a Mr. Wheeler."

"No, it wasn't a man. It was a young woman. With a *W*—Glowitz."

"That begins with a *G,*" said Berenice.

"No," said Mrs. Cork out of her muddle, now afraid of Berenice. "Glowitz was the name."

"Glowitz," said Berenice, unbelieving. "Rosie Glowitz. She's not young."

"I didn't notice," said Mrs. Cork. "Is her name Rosie?"

Berenice felt giddy and cold. The chasm between herself and Mrs. Cork closed up.

"Yes," said Berenice and sat on the sofa, pushing letters and papers away from herself. She felt sick. "Did you show her the letter?" she said.

"No," said Mrs. Cork, looking masterful again for a moment. "She told me you were repairing the flute."

"Please go," Berenice wanted to say but she could not get her breath to say it. "You have been deceived. You are accusing the wrong person. I thought your husband's name was William. He never called himself Bunny. We all call him William at the College. Rosie Glowitz wrote this letter." But that sentence, "Bring the flute," was too much—she was suddenly on the side of this angry woman, she wished she could shout and break out into rage. She wanted to grab the flute that lay on Mrs. Cork's lap and throw it at the wall and smash it.

"I apologize, Miss Foster," said Mrs. Cork in a surly voice. The glister of tears in her eyes, the dampness on her face, dried. "I believe you. I have been worried out of my mind—you will understand."

Berenice's beauty had drained away. The behavior of her one or two lovers had always seemed self-satisfied to her, but William, the most unlikely one, was the oddest. He would not stay in bed and gossip but he was soon out staring at the garden, looking older as if he were traveling back into his life: then, hardly saying anything, he dressed, turning to stare at the garden again as his head came out of his shirt or he put a leg into his trousers, in a manner that made her think he had completely forgotten. Then he would go into her front room, bring back the flute and go out to the garden seat and play it. She had done a cruel caricature of him once because he looked so comical, his long lip drawn down at the mouthpiece, his eyes lowered as the thin high notes, so sad and lascivious, seemed to curl away like wisps of smoke into the trees. Sometimes she laughed, sometimes she smiled, sometimes she was touched, sometimes angry and bewildered. One proud satisfaction was that the people upstairs had complained.

She was tempted, now that she and this clumsy woman were at one, to say to her, "Aren't men extraordinary! Is this what he does at home, does he rush out to your garden, bold as brass, to play that silly thing?" And then she was scornful. "To think of him going round to Rosie Glowitz's and half the gardens of London doing this!"

But she could not say this, of course. And so she looked at poor Mrs. Cork with triumphant sympathy. She longed to break Rosie Glowitz's neck and to think of some transcendent appeasing lie which would make Mrs. Cork happy again, but the clumsy woman went on making everything worse by asking to be forgiven. She said "I am truly sorry" and "When I saw your work in the shop I wanted to meet you. That is really why I came. My husband has often spoken of it."

Well, at least, Berenice thought, she can tell a lie too. Suppose I gave her everything I've got, she thought. Anything to get her to go. Berenice looked at the drawer of her bench which was filled with beads and pieces of polished stone and crystal. She felt like getting handfuls of it and pouring it all on Mrs. Cork's lap.

"Do you work only in silver?" said Mrs. Cork, dabbing her eyes.

"I am," said Berenice, "working on something now."

And even as she said it, because of Mrs. Cork's overwhelming presence, the great appeasing lie came out of her, before she could stop herself. "A present," she said. "Actually," she said, "we all got together at the College. A present for Rosie Glowitz. She's getting married again. I expect that is what the letter is about. Mr. Cork arranged it. He is very kind and thoughtful."

She heard herself say this with wonder. Her other lies had glittered, but this one had the beauty of a newly discovered truth.

"You mean Bunny's collecting the money?" said Mrs. Cork.

"Yes," said Berenice.

A great laugh came out of Florence Cork. "The big spender," she said, laughing. "Collecting other people's money. He hasn't spent a penny on us for thirty years. And you're all giving this to that woman I talked to who has been married twice? Two wedding presents!"

Mrs. Cork sighed.

"You fools. Some women get away with it, I don't know why," said Mrs. Cork, still laughing. "But not with my Bunny," she said proudly and as if with alarming meaning. "He doesn't say much. He's deep, is my Bunny!"

"Would you like a cup of tea?" said Berenice politely, hoping she would say no and go.

"I think I will," Mrs. Cork said comfortably. "I'm so glad I came to see you. And," she added, glancing at the closed door, "what about your father? I expect he could do with a cup."

Mrs. Cork now seemed wide awake and it was Berenice who felt dazed, drunkish and sleepy.

"I'll go and see," she said.

In the kitchen she recovered and came back trying to laugh, saying, "He must have gone for his little walk in the afternoon, on the quiet."

"You have to keep an eye on them at that age," said Mrs. Cork.

They sat talking and Mrs. Cork said, "Fancy Mrs. Glowitz getting married again." And then absently, "I cannot understand why she says 'Bring the flute.'"

"Well," said Berenice agreeably, "he played it at the College party."

"Yes," said Mrs. Cork. "But at a wedding, it's a bit pushy. You wouldn't think it of my Bunny, but he *is* pushing."

They drank their tea and then Mrs. Cork left. Berenice felt an enormous kiss on her face and Mrs. Cork said, "Don't be jealous of Mrs. Glowitz, dear. You'll get your turn," as she went.

Berenice put the chain on the door and went to her bedroom and lay on the bed.

How awful married people are, she thought. So public, sprawling over everyone and everything, always lying to themselves and forcing you to lie to them. She got up and looked bitterly at the empty chair under the tree at first and then she laughed at it and went off to have a bath so as to wash all those lies off her truthful body. Afterwards she rang up a couple called Brewster who told her to come round. She loved the Brewsters, so perfectly conceited as they were, in the burdens they bore. She talked her head off. The children stared at her.

"She's getting odd. She ought to get married," Mrs. Brewster said. "I wish she wouldn't swoosh her hair around like that. She'd look better if she put it up."

THE
SPANISH
BED

Out of the stream of cars with boats on their trailers that drive out from Colchester towards the giddy light of the sea, only one or two will turn off at a fingerpost marked To Villas. The drivers find themselves at a small house that until some twenty years ago was the home of John Osorio Grant, the novelist. It is a small place, painted in a fresh grey that gleams in the sun, rather like the silvery mud banks of the estuary when the tide is low, and is really three little villas with pinched bay windows, which Grant knocked into one somewhere about 1912 while living there for forty years with his sister. The house then passed to an enterprising man in the oyster trade who made money in a fashionable restaurant in London and was admired in the village for taking the mean little bays out of the house and putting in two long landscape windows in their place, a man greedy for views. But he tired of the country, as Londoners do, and sold the house to the present occupier, a Dr. Billiter, a retired mining engineer and mineralogist from the North who has lived a wandering working life in Chile, Bolivia and for a long time in Mexico.

The doctor is a big man, overweight, as soft as an elephant, his jacket and trousers hanging on him like a hide. He walks in a creeping way, stooping as very tall men do, as if he were following a scent, often nibbling a biscuit. In the village it is felt to be unnatural for a man of his size to be living alone. "Pure accident" he says has brought him to the village and he waves a heavy arm to give himself the careless, even frivolous air of a balloon that has slipped its mooring and taken off into the sky. What he means is that there are "pure" accidents and "vulgar" accidents; the pure accidents occur only to a scientific mind which has been long-headedly prepared for them.

He had been reading the novels of John Osorio Grant over and over again as a recreation in the lonely evenings of a life on mining sites where one gets sick of the company around one. A good detective story is like the detective work of mineralogy in a brisker, more relaxing form. His revered, though very trying mother had often kept house for him during long spells of his career and it was on the last

of his exasperating trips with her to the silver mines at Guanajuato
—where her mania for buying unwanted, picturesque rubbish in
Mexican markets was getting on his nerves—that she redeemed
herself by an astonishing discovery.

In a pile of rotting paperbacks she spotted a book called *A Visit
to the Osorio Mines.* Printed in Mexico City in 1902 and full of
misspellings, it was Grant's first book, written when he was nineteen
and had been sent out to learn Spanish by his family, who were
Osorio's agents in England. A juvenile book of fifty pages, it had
never been published anywhere else and was unknown in Grant's list
of works. The doctor became, in that instant, a potential bibliophile:
he had a treasure.

A second accident occurred—it must be an example of the "im-
pure," for it could happen to any of us—about a year before his
retirement, when he was planning to return to England and live in
the country with his mother, in one of those English villages that
are the scene of Grant's novels: places equipped with a squire, a
clergyman, spinsters, a dubious City man, a vigilant postmistress and
a house with a paneled library, gleaming with the knowledge and the
corpses it had seen. But his dear mother died. Mexico became
suddenly empty: he packed and went to comfort himself in his
dreamed-of England, but there the emptiness of his dream made
him fretful. It was at one of his lowest moments, when he was
cheering himself with a dozen oysters in a London restaurant, that
he found himself talking to the oysterman who owned Villas. The
ghost of Grant suddenly came in to occupy the empty stool beside
the doctor at the bar. In the course of a few weeks he ate dozens
of oysters and found himself buying Villas, and Grant's ghost came
down with him.

The doctor was lonely no more. From that time he talked and
hummed to himself, throbbing with the sensation that he was a
miracle. It cannot be said that he "heard" Grant telling him to put
the place back into the state it had been in *his* time, for there was
nothing mystical in the doctor; despite his slothful look, he was a
restless, practical man. He was certainly "impelled" to tear out the
blatant landscape windows the oysterman had put in, to put back
the narrow bay windows so as to darken the house, and to uncover

the stone floor that lay under the oysterman's chic parquet, as a beginning. He had always been called "the Doctor" in Mexico because of his distinction in his science; now he felt an exuberant desire for distinction in a new field. He had no friends, but he boldly created the at first imaginary Friends of John Osorio Grant Society. After a year or so they numbered about seven. They wrote to him and one or two called and he slowly got together material for a pamphlet saying that Grant was a shamefully neglected figure in the history of the detective novel, the creator of the famous Detective Inspector Coffin.

As he wrote and rewrote his sentences, a pencil drawing of Grant which he had found at a bookseller's in Colchester, looked down and seemed to say, "Enough of Inspector Coffin. What about me?" Grant had been eclipsed by his sister, the marvelous gardener and Queen of Flower Shows in local memory, just as the doctor had been dominated by his mother.

In the bluster of a spring morning another example of "pure accident" occurred. The doctor was working in the room he called his "office" which used to be Grant's study, when he heard a loud jangling noise in the bedroom above. Slates blown off? A gutter gone? Water coming through? Burglars? (On this, particularly, he was sensitive. Villas had been burgled after Grant had died.) In the manner of Inspector Coffin, the doctor went up the uncarpeted stairs to his bedroom and caught the village girl who came in to clean, bouncing saucily on the high iron bed, a decorative Spanish object with a tin panel, lacquered in black and yellow triangles at the head, and very loose, which had belonged to Grant and which the doctor had found rusting in a garden shed. Caught out, red as puberty in the face, the girl got off the jangling bed, picked up a broom and pretended to sweep the tiled floor. Shy as he was large, the doctor jerked a big thumb at the room in a general apologetic way, and went away humming.

He wished that the girl's mother still worked for him and had not pushed this impertinent daughter into the job, for she always gaped at his size, which put her into a state of swallowed giggles. But this incident changed her. From that morning she became timorous and propitiating—she was frightened that he would tell her mother.

Nervously she watched him. She was all "Yes, Doctor" and "No, Doctor." She brought him apples, she brought him biscuits—he liked nibbling biscuits, for he was a hungry hypochondriac who thought that with the exception of oysters, a square meal made him put on weight. In a week or two she came in with a Christmas card in an envelope with a long-out-of-date stamp on it.

"Very pretty," he said.

"See what it says," she said. "It was in Gran's cardboard box." Gran was long ago dead.

The doctor opened the card and then looked at the girl, who seemed to him suddenly rooted in genius or complicity. Villagers often showed him useless antiques in the hope of turning a penny or merely to show that they knew more about the place than he would ever know. Did the girl know the importance of what she had pilfered? He hoped not. But she had done what no publisher, no library, no Record Office or correspondent had been able to do. The faded ink on the card said: "Love to you, Gran dear, and all your family. Clarissa Ward." And, thank God, there was an address. He had discovered what people in the village either did not know or had forgotten, a detail which he had longed to know ever since he took the house: the address of Grant's widow.

Apart from that boyish visit to Mexico there was only one odd incident in Grant's life. As the doctor used to say lightly to any member of the Society who came to the house, "We know that he returned to England. We know that he settled here with his sister. Then there are two missing years during which, as the records show, he married a Miss Ward. Who she was, what happened to her, no one knows. The marriage lasted two years. She vanished and his sister returned. No one in the village remembers Miss Ward. "It looks as though—" he would add roguishly, "as if the two ladies did not get on. Anyway, Miss Ward seems to have been unimportant."

The word "unimportant" was slurred over. As a mineralogist the doctor believes that no fact, however small, is unimportant. Put all the facts together and one gets the whole: think of the hundreds of now precisely known facts about the formation of crystals that explain the unanswerable existence of metals. It irked him, as it would have irked Inspector Coffin, that a small fact about Grant eluded him and, as he looked at the card, he already felt the itch for an erotic secret that comes even to amateur biographers.

The doctor did nothing about the card at first, for the picture of Grant rebuked him. On the other hand, Inspector Coffin egged him on. Eventually the inspector won and the doctor sat at his type-writer, writing and rewriting a letter to Miss Ward. With a tact that seemed to him enormous and painful he said nothing about Grant. He simply wrote that he was the owner of Villas and was writing an account of the house because of its unique historic interest. He understood that she had once lived there and he would be grateful if she would consent to see him. When the letter was done, he fell into melancholy. The woman was probably dead. No reply came. After a few weeks he wrote a second letter, enclosing a copy of the first. Still no reply. Hope died. Then it occurred to him to write in his own naked hand: the clumsy personal hand, he had found, often achieved what the machine could not. He came out into the open: he said that in Mexico he had come across a little book written by John Osorio Grant which had never been published in England. He would be delighted to show it to her. This brought a reply at once from a Miss Carter saying that Miss Ward, who was seriously ill, asked her to thank him and to say she received no visitors.

Dr. Billiter rushed from his house and walked down the short rough path to the village, down the street and then up again, his face shining like the face of a euphoric but silent town crier, waving an arm boastfully. "Miss Ward, once the wife of John Osorio Grant, is alive! She exists! No one but myself knows it. You've been hiding this from me but I've found out for myself."

The only question was: Did the child know what she had done? No doubt she had eavesdropped and heard him mention the name to visitors. Still, to be certain, he bought her some sweets in the village shop. She was a hungry child.

More important was the question of the race with death. Miss Ward was old; she was ill. By the end of the week he could stand his torment no more. He set out on the drive across the middle of England to Nottingham and stood on Miss Ward's doorstep.

The house was small and trim—not in the mining or lace-making districts. He rang the bell and a small woman with grey hair pulled back painfully from a bony forehead opened the door. He jerked a thumb at the traffic and people passing in the street as if throwing them and himself away and becoming nothing.

"My name is Billiter—Dr. Billiter," he began. "I have been in correspondence with a Miss Carter . . ."

The woman looked back into the hall of the house and then gazed at him, taking in his size very much in the stupefied way of the village girl at Villas. Then she tried to enlarge herself, and in a grand voice with a tremor in it she said, "We always have Dr. Gates. Why did he send *you*? It's too late. I was telephoning all day yesterday to the hospital and in the end I had to get the ambulance myself. It is a scandal. Miss Carter is in hospital. I am Miss Ward and I shall report the matter to the authorities." At that word the small woman's neck quivered.

"Miss Ward!" cried the doctor. His thick lips parted, his mouth was wet with wonder. For a moment he wanted to pick her up and carry her off, the treasure, ten times more precious than all the silver in Mexico. "But it is *you* I wanted to see," he marveled.

She pushed her head back and looked up at him with suspicion. He saw this and spoke in his natural voice, which was as soft and polite as the buzzing of a large bee. "Miss Carter wrote to say *you* were ill and I feared—"

Miss Ward addressed the street. "I am not ill," she said. "I'm in very good health."

"I apologize for the intrusion," he said. "I happened to be passing. I am sorry to hear Miss Carter is in hospital. I really came about our correspondence. By the way, I am not a doctor."

"Then why do you call yourself one?" she said.

"Not a medical doctor. I am a mineralogist." He began to fiddle with the zipper of his briefcase. "It's about Villas," he said, appealing to her.

"What villas?" said Miss Ward. "Miss Carter is my secretary. I am not interested in buying villas or anything—"

"No," he said. "Let me explain. It's the name of my house. I am a great admirer of the work of John Osorio Grant and I am working on . . ."

He had by now got his pamphlet and the letters out of his case.

Miss Ward had bold, grey-greenish, salty eyes, and at the name
of Grant the lid of her right eye slowly drooped and closed until it
looked like a small ivory ball, and the left one like the tip of a pistol.
"There's no one of that name here. I do not let rooms," she said.
And with that she closed the door in his face. Just before it was
completely closed, he heard her say loudly to someone he supposed
to be in the hall, "Damn you."

The doctor stared at the red brick of the house. "Glazed midland
clay," he muttered, "probably a hundred years old; it never weath-
ers." It was as implacable as the woman had been. He got back into
his car, wagging his head, jerking his thumb at passing cars, humming to himself, "Poor John. Poor John." Privately he always called
Grant by his Christian name when he thought of him. John had
become part of himself, like a brother.

When he saw the village girl next day he lied to her, unnecessarily.
He said, "Yesterday I had to go to London."

One of the small annoyances of receiving visitors at Villas, even
members of the Society and especially their wives, is that they are
far more interested in the garden than in the house when the
summer comes. He is obliged to listen to their botanical comments
and hear them say, "She was a wonderful gardener."

The garden has little interest for him: it had meant nothing to
John. It was the sister's empire. The doctor is proud of having filled
in the oysterman's tiled swimming pool and shows you that the old
pond reappeared afterwards from the spring which had fed the
vulgar pool. That proves a point.

"You remember the pond in *Death Among the Lilies*?" he says.

He leads you back along a brick path. The ladies say it is a pity
that the place has "been let go so wild" and crowd around some
unusual rose or lily or shrub they have detected. At the end of a brick
path they notice two statues—or rather, there are two plinths. On
one, a goddesslike figure in graceful robes is placed, rather blotched
by lichen in the face and looking ill-used and sulky. On the other
plinth there is only a pair of feet. The figure was knocked down by
the motor mower of the oysterman's gardener. The odd thing is that

visitors often tactfully avert their eyes from the feet and replace the missing statue in their minds.

"Are *they* anyone in particular?" visitors often ask.

This annoys the doctor. He dismisses the figures. No, he says, they are only ornamental. Grant's sister picked up a taste for garden statues in Italy and she bought a pair from Stillbury Manor when the Electricity Board took over the big house. She got them for a pound a piece. It is a small satisfaction to him that here he can refer to a document; he nods to the house and says, "I can show you the receipt inside." Often as he walks around he picks up a stone and throws it into a flower bed. One has the impression that he is throwing it at someone—possibly Grant's sister.

Once he gets people back into the house his eager pride comes back. He looks down, confiding, into the face of anyone who asks a question. "The last man put parquet floors down in the rooms downstairs," he says. "This is the original stone floor." He has ripped out the modern fireplaces, of course. Furniture, he says, was a difficulty. Grant's sister, they say, had one or two valuable family things —two or three of the smaller pieces had been stolen by burglars who had broken in after John's death. But Grant's taste was for the plain and useful. Chic modern wallpaper has been scraped off. Whitewash returned, good clean whitewash.

You follow the doctor's pachydermic figure. It darkens the passages or the stairs, fussing over what relics he has found and what he is going to find. He jerks a thumb as you pass a chair, a table, a rug or a picture and says "Chair" or "Table" or "Rug," and so on. He is all modesty in his passion for the obvious. Looking out of a window he may say "Garden" or "Bird in apple tree" or "Field" or "Boy kicking football." Outside of his science he has a kind of compassion for facts, hoping they may divulge something privately to him one day.

His most apologetic moment is in Grant's study—no original furniture, but it is redeemed by his collection of Grant's novels and the files and the pencil portrait. Lately he has found out that the dealer has lied to him: the portrait is not of Grant. So the doctor says "Probably Grant" and likes to think that it will somehow turn into Grant's likeness if it is kept long enough. He gets the visitors out of this room quickly to Grant's severe bedroom. This has been

perfectly reconstructed. Spanish- or Mexican-looking tiles are back
on the floor and there is the Spanish bed—the one the village girl
was caught lying on.

After the defeat at Nottingham and when the year climbed
into the summer, the doctor took to going to the sailing club,
the only place where Grant had not been effaced by his sister,
but the sole interest of the raconteurs of that place was how
much any figure of the past had drunk or what sort of boat he
had had. About this there were arguments: none could remember. To one story he did listen carefully. The tale was that Grant
had gone out one afternoon and, in classic fashion, had got stuck
on the mud in a falling tide and had had to sit there half the
night. They added that a girl was in the boat: this is a common
myth in English estuaries. Still—you never know.

Then one day—late in August—the doctor was seen skipping fast
to the post office to send a telegram.

Another example of "pure" accident had occurred. He had received a letter with a Nottingham postmark. He studied the envelope and postmark several times before he opened it. It was addressed in a large hand that rushed downhill almost off the envelope.
The letter was from Miss Ward. He raced through it, missing most
of what it said the first time, and then he read it slowly again. The
striking thing was that all the *t*'s were crossed with long lines so that
a squall of sleet seemed to be blowing across the page.

"Dear Dr. Billiter," the letter began, "I do not know if you
recollect our meeting, the other day . . ."

The other day! It was five months ago!

". . . but I do apologize for the confusion, due to the sad circum-
stances of my friend's sudden illness."

She went on to say that she would so much like to see the
pamphlet about Villas he had mentioned and thought there were
many things she remembered about the place, although it was years
since she had been there. Would he send her a copy? Or if he was
over in Nottingham, she hoped he would call.

Going over the letter once more, the doctor saw it was dated three
weeks before the postmark on the envelope. There was a postscript
squeezed onto the bottom of the page and the last word had been
crowded out:

"I am grieved to say that poor Miss Carter has d—"

Two days after his telegram, not waiting for a reply, the doctor drove to Nottingham yawning with appetite. He finished a packet of biscuits and had to stop to buy a cake before he got once more to Miss Ward's doorstep.

For a few seconds he could not believe he was looking at the same woman. The grey hair was not drawn back but was now loose and blond. She was wearing a violet jacket and bright-pink trousers which showed she had a droll little belly and was plumper and younger. He remembered meager eyelashes; now they were long. Only the drooping of the right eyelid convinced him she was the same woman. Her shoes had high heels and she had a prowling step as she led him into a pretty room at the back of the little house, and when they sat down he noticed the high-arch shoe. She gazed at him with a doll-like satisfaction and did not listen at all to his explanations and politenesses, waving them away in a chatting fashion. But when he said how sorry he was to hear about her poor friend, her voice changed and she gave a short shake of her head. "Don't speak of it," she said in a reciting voice and choosing her words sadly and carefully: "It was a stroke."

Suddenly she stopped reciting. "So you live at Villas? How extraordinary. How time passes. And you knew *dear* Ossy? Where did you meet? In Mexico?"

"Dear Ossy!" The pet name shocked him. Obviously she had not taken in what he had just told her. "Dear Ossy"—how lightly a husband is thrown away.

"John," he said, staking his claim to the man. "No. I never met him. I found his book—or rather my mother did—as I told you. I was in Mexico long after his time. I've brought the book to show you."

She merely glanced at it and put it on the table. "It's a paperback," she said. "I thought you said it was in leather—valuable."

"Oh, but it *is* valuable: a rarity. These things are often worth a great deal."

"How much?" she said. "Thousands?"

"Oh no, not thousands—perhaps fifty or a hundred. I wasn't thinking of the money."

"You should," she said and began to wag her foot up and down. Afterwards he remembered the sudden small frenzy of her foot and, once more, that drooping eyelid that gave him the impression he was talking to two women at once.

"Anyway," she said and the eye opened, "you live in that awful house, those mean miserly little windows! And those stone floors! It was so damp! It was ruining his books—he'd lived there for years. The chimney smoked too. Poor Ossy, he ought to have been a priest. But I heard some rich man bought the place and made a lot of improvements, made it fit to live in. Ossy was very—you know—close."

The doctor was annoyed to hear his dream attacked. "I've put the bay windows back. They give the place its date—1820—its character. And the stone floors too; of course, I put in a damp course. I wanted it to be as it was in John's time," he said stoutly. And he went on to describe all the things he had done, room by room, until he saw again that she was not listening to him but studying him in detail, with a pleased ironical flirtatious smile on her face. She interrupted him.

"Does your wife like it?" she said. "Are you married?"

"Oh no, not actually," said the doctor, finding himself to his surprise apologizing.

"Why do you say 'not actually'?" She laughed. "I mean, it's not my business," said Miss Ward.

The biographer did not like being questioned. He jerked a thumb at his life as he did at things. He explained about his mother.

"Those mothers!" she said. "Was she an invalid?"

He decided to stop her questions and to get *his* life out of the way as quickly as possible by a comic exaggeration. "She had enormous, one might almost say preposterous, good health. Her death was a shock." For he himself still felt an emptiness he was fighting to fill.

"It's so unfair. It leaves guilt. One is always a prisoner," she said and her little mouth—a spoiled mouth, he thought—slipped at the corners. Then she brightened.

"You know, Ossy and I were only married two years," she said invitingly. "I do not use his name."

"Yes, I gathered . . . I was going to ask you . . ."

"The traffic is terrible in this street. Can't you hear it, even at the back?" she said to the walls of the room.

"I can't say I do."

"Humming?" she said.

This worried her, but defying the traffic, she burst out with: "Two years! When I heard he was dying—I used to keep in touch with old Granny Blake in the village, I always sent a card every Christmas, she was really the only friend I had there—I felt I had to go and see him. Even after all those years one has a picture of people in one's head. I made Miss Carter drive me there. She tried to stop me, but I just had to go. Isn't that strange? After all, he had been my husband, in spite of everything, but leave that alone. It was really shocking—big gaps in the shelves in his library where I waited. Those stone floors. His sister wouldn't let me go up at first. She told Miss Carter I was drunk. I had to force my way upstairs. Miss Carter made her let me go. That room, that horrible bed—you know he had a terrible Spanish bed?—it was the bed that shocked me and the bedclothes had not been changed. He had died two hours before and, you won't believe it, they hadn't closed his eyes. Ossy was a big man, like you, and now his body was like an insect's. His teeth! He couldn't have minded if I was drunk, could he?"

Dr. Billiter murmured. The stern Miss Ward he had met the first time appeared and the enameled face cracked at the mouth into the lines of her age.

"If his sister had looked after him instead of that filthy garden, he wouldn't have died like that," she said violently. "And the roses smelled. There was no air. I couldn't stay in it. I went outside, walked among her rotten flowers in the rain."

The passion of Miss Ward startled Dr. Billiter. He had come for a pleasant biographical chat. There were so many things he wanted to ask her about the house if only she would let him direct the conversation.

"I'll show you something," she said and went to an album which was lying on a table and put it on his knee. There was an old picture of a boat lying on the hard and John, a big man with a heavy moustache and wearing a yachting cap, was standing with his arm around a young girl—herself. He had a rudder in his free hand.

"His sister," she said, "wouldn't go near the water. Not after he got stuck on a mud bank all night with her once."

"Ah now," said the doctor. "I remember hearing—"

"He didn't love her. He loved me," she said.

This is embarrassing but better, thought the doctor nervously.

"I can prove it," she said. "Come here." And she made him come to the French window that looked out onto a small paved garden with ferns planted against the walls and a pool with lilies in it. In the center of the pool stood a stone figure.

"Ossy got Sidney McLaughlin to go it. Do you know his work?"

"I'm afraid I don't. You mean he did the statue?"

"Of course," she said. "It's me—soon after we were married."

"Very nice. Very pretty," he said politely.

"When I left his poor body in that room I walked up the path —you know the path, you must do—and there it was. He hadn't moved it. He'd kept it. After everything—bad things! That is love, isn't it?"

"You mean at Villas?" said Dr. Billiter, so embarrassed by this talk of love that he had not been looking at the figure but at the paving, noting that it was sandstone. And then the meaning of her words hit him.

"At Villas. Of course," she said.

Dr. Billiter looked closely at the figure and became flabby with unbelief. He studied the figure in every detail. With scarcely any doubt the figure was the one missing from the plinth in his garden and he fingered the catch on the window. Or was it a copy? Perhaps these ornamental figures were manufactured by the score. He could not speak. He glanced at Miss Ward and saw she was watching him with a look, half complacent, half cunning, a look that brought the village girl who worked for him to his mind. He had to struggle against his whole training and nature, against years of looking at rock and automatically naming it. Miss Ward was a deluded woman. He could not say to her, "I'm afraid you're mistaken or someone has taken you in. That figure is not you, it's one of a pair of ordinary ornamental figures that came from the garden at Stillbury Park. John's sister bought them. I've got the invoice in my papers."

"Of course I was young," she was now reciting calmly. "Long

dresses had just come in for the evenings and one wore one's hair long and tied like that."

The doctor was helpless. Painfully he allowed himself to split in two. He allowed himself to drift away with her into fantasy. "You must feel very happy to be remembered. It's charming."

"And so *like,*" she insisted. "You can see." And she fetched the photograph and made him look again at it.

There was not the slightest resemblance between the face and body of the statue and the fat girl with short black hair and wearing a heavy jersey and clumsy gumboots.

She must be mad, he thought. There was only one truth he could tell. "You have solved a mystery for me," he said. "I've often wondered what happened to the statue—you know, there is only the plinth there now, only the feet . . ."

"What feet? It's got feet," she said indignantly.

"I've asked everyone in the village what happened to it. No one knew."

"Who did you ask?" she said sharply.

"Everyone. Gardeners. Builders," he said. "The pair must have looked rather nice together."

"The pair?" she said. "There was only me. No one else."

Oh God, thought the doctor. I suppose people see only what they want to see.

"Anyway," he said, "it's the best piece of news I've had for a long time. To know it's safe. It's wonderful it came to you."

"He left nothing to me."

"Or perhaps his sister . . . ?" he suggested.

"His sister!" She laughed at that. "*You* didn't know her."

The doctor made a last attempt. "In the sale after he died?" he asked.

Miss Ward now laughed victoriously. Her fingers nipped his jacket by the sleeve and she drew him from the window. As he moved towards his chair she pulled his cuff tight and her fingers pinched as she made him flop beside her on the sofa. She leaned closely to him. "I stole it," she whispered.

"I don't believe you!" said Dr. Billiter as playfully as he could in his heavy way.

"I did. I stole it."

"A heavy thing like that," he teased. "You couldn't."

"I have *friends,* " she said. And then she became querulous, talking to herself rather than to him; this talking, as if to someone else in the room, was one of the irritations in listening to her. She was saying, "Ossy's family said, 'Who are her people? Who are her friends?' " And then openly to him: "Who wants people? I have *friends,* very good friends, very close friends.

"Oh, it would make a wonderful story for your book! His sister shut up the house but she forgot one thing—you can't shut up a garden! It was screamingly funny. I won't tell you *who* they were, but they were *friends*! They got into the garden at night by the back lane and pulled it out—into their car, of course. I can't go on calling you Doctor—what do *your* friends call you?"

"James," he said, hating to give it to her.

"I shall call you Jimmy," she said. "Jimmy. It's such a thrill—stealing, don't you think? I bet you like stealing things?"

"I suppose the nearest I've come to it is forgetting to return a book. Sweets, of course, when I was a boy," he said.

"There you are!" she said. "You must call me Clarissa. When you were in the mines in Mexico, didn't you steal silver?"

"Of course not, Clarissa"—another surrender there—"it's just lumps of crystal."

"I would have!" she cried.

He was on the point of giving her a small lecture on the crystalline origin of ores, of striation, the seaping of water, the dead pressure of rock for hundreds of thousands of years—the knowledge was at his fingertips, but the faculty for uttering facts had left him. He was adrift in her imagination. There was a vacancy in his mind, and out of it, as her fingers pinched him, his mouth spouted one of the rare and reckless inspirations of his life. "You were not *stealing,* " he said. "You were only taking what was your own."

"Yes," she said firmly.

"You were," he said, "taking yourself."

The moment he said this he couldn't believe that he had been capable of saying a thing so nonsensical and so cruelly untrue.

Miss Ward let go of his sleeve and moved away to look at him with wonder, a pretty wonder in which there was a tinge of morbid seductive gloom, like a shadow setting off a brilliant light. "You are a very clever man, Jimmy," she mumbled gravely. "I'm so grateful to you. It's a long time, so long, long and long since I have been able to open my heart to someone who understands. I can *talk* to you. I'm so glad you've come." She jumped up. "We must drink to it! What will you drink? Champagne? Yes, let us have champagne— but you'll have to open the bottle. I can't stand noise." She put her hands to her ears.

"It's rather early," said Dr. Billiter.

"It isn't! Don't move. I'll get it."

He watched her walk out of the room and feared the prowl of her arching feet. He went to the French windows and once more his fingers went to the catch. Secretively he opened the door and stepped into the little flagged garden and looked closely at the figure. Now there was absolutely no doubt: the figure was not a copy, it *had* certainly come from Villas. The feet—left behind—had been replaced and were awkwardly held to the figure by a rusting iron band. The "friends" had been in a hurry and careless, if what she said was true: there was a repaired crack across the waist. Very likely they had had to carry the statue in two pieces. His mind was wandering into the sadness of a hopeless lust and his hands itched. Morally the thing belonged to Villas and to him. He felt ashamed, now that he was alone, that he had not spoken out. Why should the delusions of others paralyze one's own desires? Why does one give in? A fantasy of his own jumped into his mind. He saw himself telling her the truth, bringing her to her senses. She gave in and begged him to take the thing, generously he offered her money—she refused— he wrapped the statue in sacking with his own hands, roped it, cased it, carted it into his car and saw the amazement of the village as, in a self-disparaging way and not to injure her—mustn't do that—he would say that he had managed to find the figure in some garden shop or stone mason's. In some way, John applauded . . .

The dream exhausted him. He heard Miss Ward's steps. He went back to the room. At least now, he hoped, they would settle down and he could ask her more questions.

"I was having another look at *you*," he said, nodding to the garden, astounded to hear himself giving in to her once more as, carefully putting a napkin over his hand, he removed the wire from the cork of the bottle.

She put her hands to her ears. "I don't think you were a miner or whatever you call it, Jimmy," she said. "I think you've been a waiter. Is it over?"

"There," he said. And slowly poured out a glass.

"You're so attentive," she said. "I'm sure your real name is Charles. You were at the old Café Royal!"

"That's right!" He laughed. "And you ordered *quenelles de brochet.* I remember it like yesterday."

"Now you are making fun of me," she said severely.

Oh dear, she was beginning again.

"I am not. To the two goddesses," he said, raising his glass to her and to the figure.

"Whew!" she said when she drank and held out her glass for more. "You are a strange man," she said and her eyelid drooped. "Tell me truthfully"—she spoke of truth-telling as an abnormality —"why are you writing about Ossy, the house and everything? Changing it. Digging out that old Spanish bed?"

"I like doing things," he said. "That bed was a find."

"Not for Ossy," she said. "Not for me." She made a prudish horrified face. "It clattered! The noise!" she said. "I wasn't in love with him. He took me from my friends. I told you I had friends, a lot. He was years older than me and his sister watched me. If I was on the telephone, she always listened behind the door."

The doctor was not sure that *he* ought to listen to her. And he wished she had not brought in the champagne.

"*I* know why you took the house. Why do you want to be Ossy? Why do you want to be someone else? Did you do something"— she pouted—"*wrong* in Mexico? I mean—police?"

"Indeed not!" he said shortly.

"I did," she said proudly. "Ossy went off to Holland on the boat and I didn't want to go. I sold all his books, his father's books, while he was away—the valuable ones, I mean."

"I don't believe you," he said.

"Don't pretend to be stupid," she said. "Four thousand pounds.

Well, he didn't give me any money. And other things too."

"I still don't believe you," he said.

"So I know why you have come here. You want to take my statue away. Someone told you I'd got it. You want to put it back on those horrible feet in your garden. I saw it when you were looking at it. That is why you kept writing letters, isn't it? Why do you keep on humming?" Her voice was becoming a shout.

He had never seen suspicion, despair and anger so suddenly splinter a face so that she turned into the old woman he had seen on the step the first time. Her face was crackling like stone and then, to his eyes, there was the mica-like glister of tears on it.

She dropped her glance to the floor and put her hands to her ears. "Stamp, stamp, stamp," she shouted like a soldier.

"Clarissa," he said. "Please. I've not come for your statue. I told you I did not know it was here."

She took her hands from her ears. "What did you say? Feet are stamping," she appealed to him.

"I said I haven't come for your statue."

"Yes you have. Why don't you take *me*, not that thing. Take me back to Villas with you. I'm in prison here." The eyelid did not droop: both eyes stared at him. "But you won't take me, will you? Oh no, you're frightened," she said slyly.

He was indeed frightened and appalled when she got up, thinking she was going to rush at him, but instead she went pathetically to the door and her hand struggled with the handle. Outside in the hall she called out, "Miss Carter. Miss Carter."

"She is mad," the doctor said aloud; "she is calling to the dead. She has got my book in her hand."

He lumbered after her. What does one do with mad women? Shake them? Startle them? Shock them by an enormous shout? She was going up the stairs, holding on to the banister. One shoe had fallen off and, out of politeness, he picked it up.

"Clarissa!" he bellowed. "You've got my book."

And following her cautiously, fearing he might have to grapple with her, he heard a door open above and saw a frail old woman in a dressing gown looking over the banister. She was carrying a stick.

"What is it, darling?" the old woman said in a voice like a man's.

"Why are you dressed up like that? You know it's forbidden." And dropping her stick, gripping the rail and in pain, one arm useless, the woman he had been told was dead grunted down the stairs.

"The police have come," Miss Ward sobbed. "Help me."

The old woman stopped and called out, "You are Dr. Billiter. I told you not to come here. Look what you've done. Stay where you are."

Miss Ward reached the old woman, who put her arm around her and said, "There, darling. It's all right."

"Let me help," said Dr. Billiter. "I understood—"

"Go away," called the old lady. "She needs me. You don't understand. Please go. Go at once."

"She said . . ." the doctor began. "She has my book . . ."

"I know what she said," the old woman said. "You're a naughty girl, darling, dressing up like that. You know that as long as I am alive I'll look after you."

"He's trying to take me away," Miss Ward whispered. "Make him go. I haven't done anything." She let the book drop from her hand.

"You can do one thing," the old woman called over Miss Ward's head to Dr. Billiter. "You can ring Dr. Gates. The number's in the red book in the front room. He knows."

And the old woman sat on the stairs holding Miss Ward as Dr. Billiter crawled up after the book and put the shoe down. "Shoe," he said out of habit and went down to the telephone.

When he came back and stood on the linoleum in the hall, he saw there was no one on the stairs. The house was silent. He waited and then he tiptoed to the door and went out into the street and stood still, breathless, not knowing where he was, until he saw his car. It was a long time before he could recall how to drive it and where he was going, and when the cars raced past him, heading for God knows where, and as the fields and trees and towns lurched at him as if they were going to vomit over him, he could only think: Carter alive! Carter alive! He rustled the biscuit bag in his pocket, but could not eat. Three hours on the road! Turned sixty as he was, he wished his mother were fulminating beside him. When at last he got to Villas, its windows catching the sea-light of the evening, the sight calmed him, but once he was inside he was scared by the speechless doors in the rooms. He could not rid himself of the feeling that they were closed against him, that the place was not his and that Clarissa Ward would open them and even John himself would be in his study, laughing at his notes and files.

That night he did not sleep in the Spanish bed. In the morning, looking out of the spare-room window at the back he saw the empty plinth. Pointlessly he waved an arm at it, and then, at nine o'clock, the village girl came.

"When I come yes'day," she said, accusing him, "you wasn't there."

She had uttered, it seemed to him, a profound truth.

A month or so later there was a letter from Miss Carter enclosing a cutting from a Nottingham paper: "Sept. 17th, Clarissa Ward, *tragically* . . ." He knew what the word meant. She had wanted that tragedy to occur at Villas!

THE
WEDDING

The market was over. Steaming in the warm rain of the June day, the last of the cattle and sheep were being loaded into lorries or driven off in scattered troupes through the side streets of the town which smelled of animals, beer, small shops and ladies. The departing farmers left, the exhaust of their cars hanging in the air.

Tom Fletcher, the forty-year-old widower with a willful twist of chestnut hair over his forehead where the skin had a knot of intention in it, drove off but got out at the open door of The Lion, and putting his head down as if threatening to charge into the crowd there, shouted, "Come on, Ted. Leave the women alone till Saturday," and Ted Archer came out and sat very tall in the car.

"That used to be a terrible place," Archer said. "The new people have done it up."

The pair drove twelve miles on the Langley road around the bottom of Scor, the hill which stuck up in a wooded lump over the slates of the town. To children of the town, Scor looked like the head of an old man, and that image sank into their minds like a kindness when they grew up. They thought the quarry carved out of the hill was his mouth. Today the rain ran off the woods into the streams that waggled below him.

Driving up the long rise to Poll Cross, the two men saw a woman come out of the larches, straight in the back and walking fast. She carried her head well.

"Effie Thomas must be hard up for it—going up the woods on a day like this," said Ted.

"Bugger," said Tom. He had the sly voice of someone enjoying a meal. "Someone got his knees wet. What's the matter with you, Ted? That's not Effie, with a back like that. That's Mrs. Jackson, the little bitch from the College, Mary's teacher. I'd give ten pounds to anyone who'd take her up Scor on a Sunday afternoon and pull her tights down. Filling my girl with a lot of parlez-vous. What's the good of French? Bugger, you can't talk French to your Herefords, Ted. Why don't you marry that teacher, Ted?"

"She's been married once already," said Ted.

"I know she has. She'll miss it, won't she then?" said Tom.

They caught up with her and made her skip up on the bank. The young woman had a rude look—very alluring.

"Jump in, you're getting your pretty hair wet, Mrs. Jackson," said Fletcher, very courtly. "Get in the back. We'll drop you. You'll be all right. I've got Ted in the front with me and I've tied his hands."

"I have been enjoying my constitutional; but, well, thank you. Yes, I will avail myself . . ."

"Avail yourself of everything while you can. We dropped the pig at the market."

"How do you do, Mrs. Jackson," said Ted when she got in and they drove on.

"Hear him?" said Tom. "He speaks French. You ought to see his heifers go off round the fields when they hear him. Like a horsefly under their tails."

"I can believe it," said Mrs. Jackson, who had a strict habit of giving a shake of her head for the sake of boldness. Fletcher was watching Mrs. Jackson in the mirror. Her fair hair was drawn straight back from her forehead into a bun at the back. It was the kind of hair that frizzes and is almost white. She was a thin, plain young woman; her blue eyes were small.

"You'll be coming to the wedding, missus, Saturday?" said Fletcher.

"I am looking forward to it," she said. "Most kind of you to ask me." Her pretty voice was cooled by all the knowledge in her head.

Fletcher dropped into country speech and said to Ted, "Tha was at school with me, warn't 'e, Ted? He's nobbut a rough farmer's boy, missus. Remember, Ted, poor old Lizzie Temple? Us dropping peppermints down her blouse?" And then to Mrs. Jackson: "He'd begun already. That's thirty-five years ago. Never ride in the back of a car with him."

"I will think of that when the temptation occurs," Mrs. Jackson said.

"When the temptation occurs. Did you hear that, Ted?"

Mrs. Jackson said she had never seen the country so green and Tom said he had never seen Mrs. Jackson's cheeks so blooming, which was a fancy, for she was as pale as a bone and her humor was dry.

They arrived at her little cottage, which stood back from the road on a short rise, and when she got out she thanked Fletcher and in her firm way she said, "I haven't given Mary up." The little blue eyes were determined.

Tom Fletcher gave one of his loud laughs and called to her as she crossed the road, "Run in quick, missus, or Ted'll chase you upstairs."

But when they drove off Ted said, "I can't stand so much forehead in a woman."

"It's the best part," said Tom. "But you wouldn't know that. But she's putting ideas into my Mary's head. It was all poor Doris's doing, sending the girl to a snobby college like that and now they want to send her to Oxford. Before Doris died I couldn't say anything, could I? But Doris has gone now. And Flo's getting married. I'll be alone in that house now, Ted, if I let Mary go."

"That's right, Tom. You will."

"It's all right for you, Ted, you dirty bugger, but I don't want my girl putting on airs and marrying a French professor. Where's the economics of it? Your family and mine, Ted, have farmed this land for two hundred years, haven't they? That's what I call economics. I want my girl at home talking English. And doing the wages. I've told old Mother Jackson so."

"How old is Mrs. Jackson?"

"Too old for you, Ted, you old bugger. Turned thirty, but I tell you if she hadn't been a friend of Doris's, I wouldn't have had her in the house, talking that classy stuff to Doris all day, about Louis IVth, the pair of them—they did, Ted, as if they were married to him. She wanted us to call one of my bulls Napoleon . . ." Fletcher's temper blew away into laughter. "No, I haven't anything against her. She's got a head on her. It's an education to listen to her. But her husband made a poor job of her. Ask me—she never had it. She sent me the bloody forms to fill up. I've got enough forms. Well—she's not going to get Mary."

They got to Ted's place and they went in to see the boxing on television. It annoyed Tom that although Ted hadn't got *his* money (for he often calculated that), Ted's house was a fine white place, fit for a gentleman, with peaches on its walled garden, well run.

"You bachelors look after yourselves," he said.

There was not a scratch on the paint inside the house, not a smear on the mahogany. If Ted hadn't won as many prize cups at the shows as he had, there was not a speck on his carpets. There were portraits of Ted's grandfather and grandmother on the wall of the dining room; the decanters sparkled. A lot of money had gone down the drain in Ted's family, but the dining table could seat twenty-five and looked as if it was waiting for the whole tribe of Ted's forebears to come back and throw away more money if he reformed and got married.

"My place has been let go since Doris died," he said jealously as he watched the boxing. "Old Mrs. Prosser comes in but she's past it. That was a low one, see that?"

They were watching the middle of a fight.

"It will be all right after the wedding," said Ted.

"All right? What d'you mean? I'll be alone in the house like you, you bugger. His eye's cut."

"Mary's a good girl. She's got brains," Ted said. "You'll have to look around, Tom."

"Look at that—footwork, footwork. The lad'll never get anywhere with that. Hit him, boy. Look around? You haven't left much around, have you, you old sod."

"There's old Mrs. Arkwright. You'll have to do a deal," said Ted slyly.

"Bugger that for a deal," said Tom. "She's had one of my tractors for a month up there. I'd sooner old Mrs. Doggett. If she was twenty years younger, I'd have her. You remember how you lassoed her at Bill Hawkins' wedding? The old girl's got a kick on her."

"She did the cancan," shouted Ted, getting a drink. "I bet your Mrs. Jackson can do a cancan. She's been in Paris."

The laughter stopped. A mean look came into Fletcher's face. "She's been divorced," he said. He stuck out his lip. "They oughtn't to have a woman like that in the College. All the la-di-da did it. But we all know who she is."

"Old Charlie Tilly's daughter," said Ted.

"The seedsman who used to have The Lion till he drank it dry," said Tom.

"News travels," sighed Ted. "There was no money there. She ran off with some society man."

"If I'd been Charlie Tilly, I'd have tanned her arse. She never told him, just ran off and they didn't see or hear of her for twelve years," said Tom.

"Mrs. Tilly didn't know anything until she saw a picture of her in a magazine at the dentist's—all dolled up at Ascot races. High society," said Ted.

"And comes back here as if nothing had happened."

They sat in silence and then Fletcher said, "She ran through twenty thousand pounds of her husband's money." He swelled with satisfaction at the size of the sum and at the thought that a local girl could do that. "She's got a brain. Ah now, look at that—he's marking him."

They watched the fight to the end.

Messell the art master at the College came into Mrs. Jackson's study. It had once been the housekeeper's room in the large country house which the College rented. For five years since she came out of the hospital after her divorce and the rest of her scandal, she had been teaching here.

Messell said, "What's the matter with the town bull's daughter, Christine? I've just passed her in the corridor wiping her eyes."

Mrs. Jackson considered Messell for a while. "Her sister is getting married. She is quarreling with her father. I am going to the wedding," she said.

"It's this place," said Messell. "It's too grand for them. How many of them have got ballrooms forty feet high with painted ceilings in their homes? They walk about dreaming they are duchesses."

Messell was wearing a cape and a violet tunic done up with small buttons high on the neck, and there his round face rested on it like a detachable moon. His large round eyes were vain of their woes. It would be no surprise, she thought, to see him carrying his head in his hand, for he had the look of one wishing he had been executed in more dashing times than the present.

"Speak for yourself," she said in her bossy way. "Why shouldn't they think they are duchesses? I always wanted to be one. Girls are practical. A girl is a new thing: they have to invent themselves."

"Did you invent yourself?" Messell said.

"Of course," said Mrs. Jackson.

Messell had the prowling gaze of one who is vain of seeing through people.

"Why," he asked, "why did we leave London for a dump like this?"

"We?" she said. "I have to earn my living. What are you going to do this half-term?"

It was impossible to get anything out of Mrs. Jackson.

"Sleep," he said. "Drink. What are you going to do?"

"I told you I'm going to the wedding tomorrow," she said.

"Why are women so mad about weddings?" he sneered.

"We live for the future," she said. "Why don't you go to London and commit a sin?"

The sun was beginning to shimmer in the summer mists next morning as she drove towards the town.

When she had first come to teach at the College, five years ago, she was uneasy at the sight of the countryside she had left when she was a girl and rarely left the park that surrounded the place. She did not want to be seen. But after a year she drove defiantly into Langley; she had to face it. It was enemy country: the enemy was her childhood. When she saw Scor hill coming boldly out of the summer haze, and the slate roofs of the town in its hollow, every house, every window flashed old dull hatreds. In time they vanished and became no more than a tale—for the place emptied. The people in the shops and in the streets looked unreal. She seemed at once a ghost and yet the only real and living person there. It annoyed her that the people she passed and looked at so intensely did not ask to know who she was. She compelled herself on one of these early visits to stand in front of The Lion, where her father had brought her to live when she was six and he had married again. It was a mean little place but it sparkled now, and she looked at the top bedroom window at the front where she had so often stood, outstaring the dry, Biblical brick of the Baptist chapel opposite, a building that seemed to forbid the thoughts in her head. It now looked feeble; she had outwitted it. How much shouting had gone on in the family. How proud she had been her name was Tilly and not the name of her handsome stepsisters, whose beauty had looked greedy and common to her. They had grown up and married now. The only unmarried one was living in another pub at Fenn twenty miles away, with her stepmother.

After one long compelled stare she did not visit the place again, but when she went to the town nowadays her ghost at the window of the place eyed her from the street she avoided. Guilt gave way to a new regret which went on for years—that she had never brought her husband to see the place where her plots and ambitions were born, because she was afraid. Once, on one of her low evenings this last year, she had been on the point of telling Messell her story, for in his prowling way he had sniffed out that she was a fellow casualty, but she stopped herself. He was not up to it. He was muddy with remorse about something: he lacked the secret pride of prodigals and had stopped at dressing up.

Today as she drove, Scor hill came up stealthily. She parked her car and went into the church she had not been in since she was a child. It looked smaller, of course, and the Latin inscriptions on the tablets of the stone walls seemed nearer. She read one, looking for howlers out of habit. The organ dribbled out a squealing flourish, and for a moment she could hear her husband's voice calling to her in that church at Toulon on their honeymoon: "Here's one! Look at this." They were looking for the tomb of Comte de Tillet. The Tillys were French émigrés! she had told him. The unforgivable thing about him was that he had the innocence of the rich and accepted her fantasies as a compliment to himself. But now the organ bellowed as if from all Tom Fletcher's herds, and Fletcher walked up the aisle with Mary's sister, the bride. He marched forward, correctly in step, with his crested head lowered, chin forward on his short strong neck, his brow knotting when his eyes marked the site of the altar as if he would pause to pad his feet and lower his shoulders and gallop the last three yards, catch the vicar and send him flying in his surplice. Yet he stopped with the ease of a man at the market.

"Doesn't it strike you," she wanted to say to the congregation, to keep her distinction, "doesn't it strike you as all rather indecent?"

But her question was sung down by the hymns, particularly by an aunt of the bride who was sitting behind her and by an uncle as pink-skinned as a salmon. The restiveness of the ceremony got into her waist and legs, and afterwards when she left the church she was smiling and excited by the chatter outside. She drove on to Fletcher's house and felt, for the first time since her divorce, unmarried. The eyes of the other women sparkled with the same brief hungry feeling themselves.

There was the marquee striped in red and white on the lawn—Mary had boasted that it would be. What a day for boasting! The scene was like a flower show and between the hats of the ladies she saw the long view of the fields and woods and hills buzzing in the sun, and the cattle down below slowly moving up the fields curiously, as excited as the crowd, to the garden hedge. It was astonishing to find herself among so many tall young men whose weathered necks stuck out of their white collars. The bride was in full folly, queening it before the groom, rushing him from one group to another as though she were going to eat them all. Fletcher stood confidently among his guests, shouting in his meaty way, yet bowing—really *bowing*—to the ladies, old and young. The tuneful aunt spoke to Mrs. Jackson, and she, feeling that a fantasy of the learned kind was called for, said in a ringing voice, "Mr. Fletcher has the head of a Roman emperor."

The aunt was baffled. Mrs. Jackson explained, "As it might be on a medallion."

"He won two first prizes at Cottesbury," said the aunt, who belonged enthusiastically to contemporary life.

Mrs. Jackson repeated her remark to the vicar, who nodded, and she was inspired to develop the idea: "One forgets how much of Roman wealth must have been in cattle."

This news made the vicar anxious to move away and he adroitly introduced her to another aunt. "This is Mary's famous Mrs. Jackson," he said.

"If only poor Doris could have seen this day. This is what Tom has just said to me. It is sad. She was the love of his life," said the aunt.

That sentence rang through Mrs. Jackson's head all afternoon. At some time or other everyone in the town and the countryside would take a long breath and utter it. Ted Archer had innumerable loves of his life; her stepsisters had been thick in the gossip of these loves. On every day of the week, except the day of the cattle market, the town was enthralled by love of every kind, even when money went over the counters in shops or ladies went to the library or drank their tea. Window blinds signaled it. One looked at the unlikely people, but the sentence ran from glance to glance.

Mrs. Arkwright, coloring up with champagne in the heat and sitting in the tent on a chair that was sinking into the grass, uttered the sentence to Mrs. Jackson: "I lost my husband. He was the love of my life—I know. But we mustn't think of ourselves. It's Mary I'm worried about, losing a sister. Tom will be alone in the house. My heart bleeds for that man." Mrs. Arkwright was panting. "I'm resting because of my leg. I must get some air."

She obliged Mrs. Jackson to help her into the garden. "It's not like one of your London weddings," she said. "Ah, there's Tom, poor man. As I was saying, Mary ought to get away. I'm on your side. *You* understand."

Mrs. Arkwright threw away a cigarette and coughed into the flower bed and then turned to consider the pleasant house. "It's sheltered," she said, lighting another cigarette and giving a pull to her waist, for she was large, boxed into her clothes, dark-haired and brimming with fate. "He's letting it go. I don't mean anything nasty, but the sitting-room paint! And then upstairs—you can see for yourself there's no woman. And Mary at the College: she is too young. Of course you can't say anything to *him*. But I agree with you."

Mrs. Jackson got away to the hedge at the bottom of the garden and Tom Fletcher came up to her.

"Is that Scor?" she said. "What a lovely view."

"Twenty miles of steak, missus," Tom Fletcher said and he called to Ted Archer, "Come here, you bugger. Mrs. Jackson wants you to take her up Scor hill."

"I went up there when I was a child," said Mrs. Jackson primly.

Fletcher sent out one of his bellows of laughter. "I never met a woman here who hasn't," he shouted and gave Ted Archer a punch.

The afternoon moved on from laugh to laugh. There was silence for a speech about the secret of happiness. The bride laughed and pouted. The groom said, "All I can say is, she is a smashing girl. She's the love of my life." And that over, the men got into groups and talked about their farms and the children played hide-and-seek around the skirts of the women as the afternoon lolled in the fields and Scor became plainer and nearer, creeping up like the cattle. At last the women moved to the front door of the house, waiting for the couple to come down, and one or two young men shouted up at the window, "Come on, Jim, can't you wait?"

Three men went into the drive to the car under the dusty elms and the young children now climbed on to the flint wall by the yard, the girls grabbing at the legs of the boys. The afternoon wheeled and cooled; short shadows edged their way out from the trees. Mrs. Arkwright came slowly across the lawn and pushed her way to stake a claim in Fletcher in the crowd by the door. There was a scrimmage, the confetti flew, the photographers calmed them all down, there was a click as time stopped. Then shouts. Tom Fletcher went down with Mary and the couple to the car and he picked up a child that had fallen on the way. Ted Archer blew his hunting horn and off went the car and young men slapped on the roof. As it crawled out on to the lane a man suddenly scrambled on top of the roof and was carried away, banging violently on top of it. A bottle fell from his pocket and broke on the road.

"Who's that?" said Fletcher.

But the car had gone.

Oh God, said Mrs. Jackson to herself. Messell. He's drunk. How did he get here?

The young men went into the lane and watched, and after a long time, back came Messell without his cape, in his violet shirt, covered in dust and a trouser leg torn.

"It's all right," he shouted. "I'm impotent. I want Mrs. Jackson. Where's Mrs. Jackson?" he shouted as he stumbled into the drive.

Mrs. Jackson dodged up the steps into the house. What a disaster! How had he got there? She hid in the bathroom; she could just see him swaying and talking among the men, who were looking at him in silence, and then she saw him sit on a grass bank. She came down in the large empty sitting room. It had not changed since Doris's time. All those thin silver vases! And the photographs of the shows, the smell of roses and cigarettes, and the family chairs empty. The seats had slackened since Doris's time, helplessly. Peeping from the window, Mrs. Jackson saw children watching Messell: he had got up again. She did not know where to go for safety. She went along to a room she remembered—the one Fletcher called his office. The blinds were down to keep out the sun, and in the low light she could see only the glimmer of the silver cups Fletcher had won. She went in and listened.

"Little Chris Tilly."

She stiffened at the lazy, insinuating impertinence of his voice. She had not heard her maiden name spoken for years.

Fletcher was sitting at his desk looking at his wages sheets.

"Oh, I'm sorry," said Mrs. Jackson. "I didn't see you. I came in to the cool."

"Who are you chasing?" he said.

There was suddenly loud shouting from the yard.

"Stay there a minute," he said. "I want to say a word to you."

He went out and soon came back. "Did you bring that professor with you?"

"Certainly not."

"I don't want any professors here. I've got enough trouble with government inspectors. You've got some funny people up at the College, missus."

He stared at her rudely and she set her chin.

"Well, don't go. Sit down with me. Look at all this stuff. Forms, forms, forms. Buggered if I can read them. Mary'll have to do it. Have you taught her to read forms? How to pay wages—that's what a girl needs. That's education. Well, that's where it all goes," he said and picked up the papers and dropped them into a wastepaper basket.

Mrs. Jackson smiled, but Fletcher scowled slyly.

"*And* the forms you sent me, missus. My girl's staying here. No offense, missus, but you've had your turn; now it's mine."

"Don't let us discuss it now. It's been a lovely wedding. Flo was so pretty. And such a nice young man."

"He'll do if he can make anything out of a hundred acres. If she makes him work. You can have all the professors at Oxford and Cambridge, but my girl stays here, missus, and she knows it. You've got to tell her. If she won't listen to me, she'll listen to you."

"She's got the best brain in the school," she said. "She's desperate. If you're not careful, you'll lose her altogether. Mrs. Arkwright was talking to me . . ."

Tom Fletcher reddened as he stared at her. "Old Mother Arkwright doesn't know her arse from her elbow. My daughter's my business."

"I don't think this is the time to talk about it," said Mrs. Jackson. "Mary's a prizewinner." And she waved towards the cups on his shelves. "Like you. Don't you think she should choose?"

"No," said Fletcher. "I never chose. You didn't choose."

"But I did."

"So they tell me," he said morosely. "I haven't anything against you, missus. Your life's your own. But I've got fifteen hundred acres." He looked around the room. "Look at the state those cups are in. Old Mrs. Prosser comes in, but now Flo's gone, who will clean them?"

Fletcher was himself startled by his own turn of mind. A shout from the yard disturbed him. Mary ran into the room. She stopped when she saw Mrs. Jackson and her father. "They're chasing Mr. Messell, Mrs. Jackson," she said anxiously.

"Let 'em chase him," said Fletcher, getting up. "I've said all I want to say. Let's see what the lads are doing. Us country lads like a bit of sport. This isn't your first wedding here," he shouted, and when he got up he gave her a slap on the bottom. "Come on."

He pushed Mrs. Jackson to the door, and when they got out onto the steps of the house, there were Ted Archer and two or three others, in their black wedding clothes, but now with ropes in their hands. One of the farmers had flung out his rope and lassoed another who was getting out of it, just as Archer was sending out his own rope at Messell, who dodged. In a moment three men were out for Messell, who dodged again and backed to the yard wall and then suddenly slipped through a gap at the side of it. They were after him.

Cars started up. The guests were going. The young farmers came back, followed by Messell. They were tired of him and he flopped down again on the grass bank.

The children visited him from time to time with wonder: he was stretched out asleep on the grass. Tom Fletcher winked at Ted Archer, who sent out his rope and caught one of the aunts. She screamed with such pleasure that one of the men rushed at her, picked her up in his arms and carried her to the open trunk of his car and dumped her into it as she kicked up her legs. She climbed out and her hair came down. Three other ladies doubled up with inciting laughter and mocked the men. One by one the men chased and caught them.

Tom Fletcher's red face swelled like a turkey cock's: he was shouting. "Give us the cancan, Mrs. Doggett," he shouted as the old lady's legs went up in the air. The aunt with the beautiful voice climbed out of the trunk of a car and dared them to rope her again. Fletcher stood near Mrs. Jackson and called out "Go on!" to the men. The dust flew. The skirts went up, the hair came down. Then it all stopped and the women got together, panting, tidying their clothes and now daring Tom Fletcher himself, who had picked up a rope.

Mrs. Jackson took the opportunity to go to Fletcher and in her politest manner said, "Goodbye, Mr. Fletcher. I'm afraid I have to go. I have an engagement. It has been a lovely wedding."

"Go?" he said. "You can't go."

But she went off to her little car. He watched her. He leveled the rope.

"Mrs. Jackson!" Mary called.

Fletcher's rope snaked out, knocked Mrs. Jackson's hat over her eyes and was over her shoulders, pulling her hair down and biting on her waist. He pulled her stumbling towards him.

"Daddy!" shouted Mary.

Mrs. Jackson's face hardened as she got her footing and showed her bold teeth at him. The other women had laughed when they were caught, but she did not. She pulled fiercely at the rope and she surprised him by a sharp pull that got it out of his hands. He made a grab at it and missed. He was stupefied as she stared at him. The aunts watched in silence. Slowly Mrs. Jackson got out of the rope, carefully picked it up and walked to her car. Mary rushed after her.

"Go away, child," said Mrs. Jackson, and the girl rushed back to her father with tears in her eyes and then ran into the house, red-cheeked with shame.

They saw Mrs. Jackson arranging her hair in the car mirror while Fletcher stood there scowling and silent, and everyone stared at him. Ted Archer dropped his own rope. Fletcher grinned uncomfortably and then Mrs. Jackson drove off fast. They stood listening to the sound of her car as it went over the hill behind the farm.

"Tom," said Ted Archer. "She's gone off with your rope."

Five pigeons on the roof of the house flew off in a wide circle. They seemed to be following her.

Messell got up from the grass and walked towards Fletcher. "Sir, that was not the act, that was not the act, act . . ." He could not go on.

"Bugger off," said Fletcher and went sullenly into the house, shouting for his daughter.

"Intolerable," Mrs. Jackson muttered as she drove fast to the main road, looking into the mirror to see if she was followed.

"Little Chris Tilly"—the countryside had broken its long silence about her; he was mocking her, all those ridiculous women, so polite to her face, were mocking her. She did not mind, but to be roped in like that, by a man, with the lot of them, was too much. She could feel the blow of the dirty rope on her neck, feel its bite on her waist and see the dusty marks on her dress, and despite her temper she felt weak. She looked in the mirror again and again, feared still that she was followed and could not get his stare, as he threw the rope at her, out of her head. The fear was strong enough to make her get off the main road and take the long way home, looking for some private place where she could straighten her clothes, and when she found one she stopped her car and went nervously into the trees and pulled up her dress to see whether her skin was marked. There were no marks.

"All the same!" she protested and drove on more calmly and she was left with impatience at the girl's tears.

"She'll have to fight for herelf," she said. "I did. After this I'm not going to raise a finger for her. Anyway, she'll fall for the first man she sees and that will be the end of her."

The evening clouded as she sat restlessly in her cottage trying to read and stopping to look from the windows as each car went by, and at last went into her back garden. The air was heavy, the trees were darkening and still. There was a large elm in the field beyond and it was oppressive in its huge, spreading silence, waiting.

She sat in a deck chair watching the grass grow dimmer. Presently an inexplicable eddy of wind passed across the field until, striking the elm, it swirled into the tree, lifting and parting the branches as if men had got into it and were tearing it; it heaved and swelled and raved for a full minute and then suddenly the wind passed.

"I shall go to London. I must get hold of someone. Who shall I ring?" she said. She went indoors and got out her suitcase and began getting dresses out of a closet, holding them up and then throwing them on the bed. Only one she picked up again.

"You little tart," she said, "where have you been?" And she threw it down again. There was a knock at her door.

"Fletcher," she said and stood, all the strength running coldly out of her legs and then rushing back up her body and tossing in her heart.

"No, Messell of course," she said to deceive herself. She looked out of the window and saw a bicycle standing against the garden wall.

"It's me. It's Mary," the girl's voice called.

The girl stood white-faced and hot in the little sitting room. She said, "I'm not going back. Oh, Mrs. Jackson, I've run away. I'll never forgive him."

Mrs. Jackson made her sit down and the girl cried on her shoulder.

"It was so insulting to you," she was saying.

Why, thought Mrs. Jackson as she listened to the girl, why have I got to relive my life?

And when she said this, sensations of triumph sparkled in her and her heart was warm. Years of self-accusation vanished from her and the headlong tenderness of being young flowed in.

"But I was not insulted at all. Surprised, yes, but it was rather a compliment," she lied.

The girl looked gravely and mistrustfully at Mrs. Jackson.

"Did you tell them you were coming here?"

"No," said the girl.

"Good heavens," said Mrs. Jackson. "We must get you back at once. I'll take you. They'll be out of their minds. At this hour."

"I saw your face," said the girl.

"You mustn't go by faces," said Mrs. Jackson. She went to her bookcase and picked out a book. "This is what I promised to lend you. I was going to bring it this morning."

The girl held the book in bewilderment.

"I shall tell your father you came for the book," Mrs. Jackson said.

She told the girl to read the book while she made some tea. It was called *Rambouillet: The Art of Conversation.*

"You wrote it!" exclaimed the girl.

"Yes, I did. I was going to bring it to give it to you at the wedding, but I forgot. Better late than never."

She drove the girl back to the farm, where Ted Archer was standing at the door.

"She's here," called Archer, and Fletcher came rushing out.

"Mrs. Jackson forgot to give me this," the girl said. "I've been to fetch it."

"At this hour?" said Fletcher as Mary kissed him.

"We've been all over the countryside looking for her," said Ted Archer quietly to Mrs. Jackson as they went inside. "They had words."

They sat on the large shabby chairs and Fletcher listened silently to Mrs. Jackson's chatter about the wedding, staring at her, and when at last she made him laugh she put on a prudish, busy face and got up to go at once.

"I'll be up tomorrow for my rope," he shouted from the doorstep as she switched on the car lights and drove off. It was the only time he spoke. His shout seemed to own the night.

When she got back to her cottage, she lay on her bed. "Oh no," she said in the little hot room. A heavy night of throwing off bedclothes. Trivial dreams of voices and faces and Fletcher sitting in his chair and staring at her! And then—what a triumph—in the morning there was a mark on her waist: it had come up in the night. She would have liked to show it to him.

She had washed her hair and was sitting with a scarf around it, looking harsh and prim, when Fletcher came in the afternoon.

She put on an impudent mouth when he came to the door. She took the rope down from a hook. "Here is what you came for."

He took it and dropped it down outside on the step and then came in and sat down on the sofa.

"You've done something to this place since the old postman had it. It belonged to Randall; he was a fool to let it go. We got a bit rough, as Mary says. But I told her I could see you were on your way, and the best way to get a lady to stay is to stop her from going! I know, I know—the lads were rough."

"Well," said Mrs. Jackson. "I am not cattle. I suppose it was what one would have to call a country junket."

"I can't bear the stuff," said Fletcher innocently. "We used to give it to the girls, with prunes, when they wanted loosening."

Mrs. Jackson sat very upright on her chair.

"I had an engagement," she said.

"That's just what I said to Mary—she's been carrying on. I said you'd got an engagement."

"How is Mary?" said Mrs. Jackson.

"Girls get excited by weddings," he said. "You saw the heifers. News spreads. You've been married and so have I—it makes a difference. What's that?"

He pointed to a picture hanging on the wall beside the fireplace. It seemed to be a foam of pink cream and lace, and then he saw the vanishing chalk outline of a doll or a girl floating in the foam, possibly on a garden swing: there was a pink face, two indigo blurs for her eyes, the poppy red of a drooping mouth. The creature was either just appearing or disappearing in the paint.

"It's a Vandenesse," she said, recovering her grand voice. "French."

He nodded. "Expensive, I expect," he said.

"My husband gave seven hundred and fifty pounds for it," said Mrs. Jackson coldly.

Fletcher was silent, then he said, "A rich man."

"Very," said Mrs. Jackson.

"Yes, that's what I heard."

Fletcher shifted on the sofa. "Bugger, I sold a bull last week for two thousand pounds. Who is it supposed to be?"

"It's a portrait of the Comtesse de Tillet," she said.

He nodded. "It would look funny in a farmhouse," he said.

"Yes, but this is not a farmhouse," she said.

Mrs. Jackson gave a shake of her head to change the subject. "I was writing you a letter," she said, pointing to the table by the window where she had been typing. "But you throw letters away, don't you, so coming here you've saved me a sheet of paper. I have been thinking of what you said to me yesterday about Mary. I've changed my mind since last night. I agree with you. Mary's better off at home."

"What's this?" said Fletcher, startled. "Turnabout, I see. Are you telling me she's not good enough?"

"Oh, she's a clever girl," said Mrs. Jackson. "Simply—I was mistaken."

"You're saying she's not good enough."

"Not at all. I've changed my mind."

His face was amiable. "I'll tell you what you are, missus. You're a bloody liar." He laughed. "And I'll tell you something else. That picture's not the Countess of whatever you call her: it's you. Mary told me."

"It is the title of the picture. I have the catalogue," she said.

"It's you. Only he's taken all your bones out. He ought to have knocked something off for the price of that. When I am buying an animal I want to see how it stands. I look at its bones."

"I am sure you do," said Mrs. Jackson sharply. "But my husband was buying a work of art, not an animal. Don't you like it? The dress is very pretty, don't you think? I love the dress. I've got it upstairs. I was thinking of taking it to London tomorrow—very silly, of course, it's so out of date."

It was delightful to sit there, looking so plain, and to mock him. She got to her feet. "I'll get it," she said.

"No," he said, standing up, and he held both her arms. "Stay where you are. You and me have got to do a deal. I want you over at the farm."

"But I'm going to London. What deal? I know—you want me to clean all those cups."

"I did them myself this morning," he said intently. "I want you down at the farm and we'll do what you like about Mary."

In the cottage room the short man seemed to shut out the afternoon light. He was looking into her small blue eyes and she saw he dismissed the fight in them and in her chin. He let go of one arm and neatly pulled the scarf from her head, so that her damp fair hair straggled to her shoulders. She put on a face of horror that gave a twist to her parted lips, but the horror was growing into a pleasure in itself. It heated and was growing into a noise in her head as he stared at her, and yet in quick glances he was also taking in the room, the door, the furniture, the cushions, the books and did not even spare the rugs on the floor. His stare was the stare of the hunt.

"Sit down. Please let me go," she said.

She was astonished, she was disappointed, when he sat down.

"Tom," she said. "Me. On a farm. Are you mad?"

"You know my name, anyway," he said. "I'm not mad." And then he said simply, "You brought Mary home."

"Of course I did. What do you imagine?" she said.

"You brought Mary home," he said again.

"You don't know anything about me," she said.

"I know everything about you." He nodded at the picture. "He's got your mouth."

"My mouth?" she said. She could not resist turning to the picture and looking at it with a moment's pride, and then the horror came back into her face and she mocked again. "You go by mouths too," she said.

"Yes," he said and pulled her gently by the hand to the sofa, where she skillfully sat away from him.

"My hair is wet," she said, pushing it back over her ears. "What a sight I must be. Go on—what are you saying? You want a housekeeper? Now, there's Mrs. Arkwright—"

He did not let her finish the sentence. She was pushing his hands away, his arms, opening her mouth to speak, her ears full of din and her eyes scattering her hatred until, in a pause, her skin burned and her eyes dulled as his were dulled and her lips drooped, when his kissing stopped.

"At least," she said in a hard low voice into his coat, "at least lock the door."

There was a lot of talk at the shows that summer when Fletcher and she and sometimes Mary, too, drove off together. Ted Archer denied it all until Tom had his house repainted and Mrs. Jackson left the College and sold her cottage. Messell went about saying Vandenesse was a third-rate painter with a knack of catching girls inventing themselves but no good when they had turned thirty.

THE
WORSHIPPERS

Eeles worshipped Lavender, Lavender worshipped Eeles but worshipped Gibbs absolutely—but what is worship? It is not love. To worship is to be put in a trance by an image. There is not much time for this commodity in the rag trade in that district of London that lies infested by anxiety between the north side of Oxford Street and the Middlesex Hospital.

At eight-fifteen every morning Lavender is sulking like a middle-aged schoolboy, head down, under his bowler hat, as he walks towards his office building. He affects a hump to his shoulders, but when he gets there, or rather, when he "comes alongside" or smartly "up to moorings"—as he still says after his time in the Navy years and years ago—he lowers his shoulders and gives a sway as he turns, feeling the roll of *Ripper*, the destroyer he was in, mostly in the Channel, or the French gunboat in which he served on the Yangtze. He is wearing an expensive suit and carrying a correctly rolled umbrella. Five seconds later Eeles, who has been standing in another doorway reading a newspaper and on the lookout for his boss, slips the paper in his pocket and follows Lavender up five flights of dirty stone stairs and joins him just as he is putting his key in a door lettered LAVENDER & COOK in black on the frosted glass, and follows him into the inner office. There Gibbs, Lavender's great-uncle, is waiting for them. Gibbs has been there all night, hanging on the wall, done in oils and heavily encrusted in a gold frame, three foot three by two foot nine, first shown publicly at the Royal Academy in 1882.

Eeles, short, going bald and getting plump, but much younger than Lavender and nothing like as well-dressed, stands at attention as at an inspection of armored cars in which he served in the war, while Lavender glances at Gibbs to see whether he is hanging straight. Then both men go to their desks.

"He's much better in this room than he was when we were in the front of the building," Lavender has said more than once.

Once or twice Eeles has said, "Much better now he's been cleaned up."

Gibbs, in his eighties perhaps, is sitting with the difficulty of very stout men, at a desk. His white hair sticks up short like pig's bristles; his cheeks, chins and the roll of fat around his neck are as pink as a baby's; his little blue eyes are bright and gluttonous. Below the neck the body rests like three balloons at bursting point, the last one resting on his legs. A watch chain travels across his waistcoat like a caravan of annual profits. The whole figure has the modesty and the anonymity of pork, for—as Lavender has many times told Eeles and others—Great-Uncle Gibbs had made a quarter of a million in the bacon trade and contained, even consumed, the firm of Drake, Feldström, Gibbs and Schmidt (London, Colchester, Hamburg and Copenhagen, Ltd.,) and was the best judge of claret south of the Wash.

Eeles's worship of Lavender had begun when he first saw the portrait. The picture might be terrible, old Gibbs might be vulgar, but in him Lavender had an ancestor. Lavender was, therefore, a gentleman. Eeles decently agreed that to be a gentleman was an asset, though as one who could offer nothing like it in return, he privately thought the condition might not be worth the candle and could even be tragic. What was good for bacon was not necessarily good for the rag trade.

As for the credit side of the account, Eeles would never forget Lavender's handling of Cook. The title of the firm had become a commercial fantasy. Cook had been a nonworshipping man—a *haben Sie?* fellow, hand outstretched, as Lavender said, drawing on the three or four words of German he had picked up in the firm's connections with Frankfurt—who had suddenly cleared out two years ago taking customers with him and starting up in competition. Lavender's manner during this row reminded Eeles of Lavender's version of what happened to the officer commanding *Ripper* who, having scraped the hull of that destroyer against the wall of a Dutch harbor as a stick of bombs fell on it while getting a Royal person out safe and sound, received an engraved document from the Admiralty expressing "Their Lordships' displeasure." Lavender was a master of being as displeased as a lord, if the occasion arose.

Eeles said, "I wanted to kick the bugger downstairs."

This so pleased Lavender that his worship of Eeles began.

"S-s-so," said Lavender, who stammered a little but mastered it by pulling a face and giving an attractive twist to his neck, "s-so did I."

After Cook saw the red light and cut his losses, money was tight for Lavender and Eeles, and the firm moved into two smaller and cheaper office rooms at the back of the building. They looked over an alley where the light was dimmer but one could at any rate open a window and let what passed for air into the place. The two men cleaned up the rooms one Sunday. "Operation Removal" began. Lavender stripped to his underpants, as he had often had to do when he was Ordinary Seaman 0267etc. before he got a ring of gold braid and his commission. The dandy was surprisingly strong, hairless and in good condition, no sign of fat on him except in the jowl; with his long lashes and thick dark hair he looked like a youth. He had been a pretty child. Eeles, who was much younger but was putting on weight, took off only his shirt and jacket and was sandy-haired and very pink—as pink as Gibbs, Lavender noticed. They swept down the dirty cream walls of the two rooms with brooms, Lavender being finicky about dust, then washed them. It was Lavender who, saying he had of course scrubbed decks and cleaned grease off propeller shafts, went down on his knees and scrubbed the lino left by the previous tenant, calling out that it was "coming up" green as grass. Eeles protested at the sight of an older man like Lavender getting down on his knees—an officer too—but he remembered his major in the war who screamed like bloody hell if there was a speck of dirt on a tank. Lavender got up with his pail of filthy water from time to time and looked out of the window. He said it was a pity the street below was not the English Channel or the Yangtze. Eeles was nervous about this but controlled himself.

Then they moved the furniture. This Sunday was the most enjoyable day in the history of the firm: they talked often about it afterwards.

"Back a bit," said Eeles as they heaved the two desks from the front of the building to the back.

"Mind the bloody door handles," said Lavender, not concerned with Eeles's knuckles but with possible scratches on the wood. He was touchy about scratches. While they were lifting the metal filing cabinet two of the drawers slid open, letters and invoices showered on the floor. The two men put the thing down and picked up the papers.

"Good God, here's one from dear old Hauser," said Lavender, picking it up. In more prosperous days they had had the Hauser agency for Swiss lace but had lost it when Hauser died. The letter was written in French and Lavender started reading it aloud. Lavender had spent two years in a French silk factory, learning the trade, when he was young. Eeles did not understand French, had never met Hauser, but stood more or less at attention respectfully because Lavender's eyes were glistening with worship.

"After he died I stood outside Le Coq au Vin where we had dinner every time I was in Lausanne and I cried like a child," he said. He had worshipped Hauser, Hauser's wife, Hauser's daughters and their husbands.

Eeles nodded his head and said to break the emotional moment, "Now we come to the big stuff."

There were heavy rolls of lace, brocades, and so on, eight feet long. To heave this dead weight down the corridor from the old office was like lifting dead bodies. There was nothing to grip. One had to cuddle the damn things. Lavender put his hand to his back. When he was a boy a Gibbs cousin of his, he said, had pushed him off a tree and he had nearly broken his back: he often got twinges there even now. Still, he did his part. After four in the afternoon the job was done except for the most important thing: hanging the picture of Great-Uncle Gibbs.

It was disturbing when you thought about it, Lavender said, that an old man who must have weighed two hundred and fifty pounds in life should weigh so little in a portrait, even allowing for the frame. A relief—as Eeles said. But to get at the right height on the wall above Lavender's desk called for ruler and pencil marking, arguments about the exact spot, Eeles holding the picture up for Lavender to consider and Lavender holding it up for Eeles, who said eventually, as his arms ached, that the old man had come to life and was making his weight felt. An hour passed before the wall was plugged and the picture was hung.

When they had washed and dressed they came back to the room and considered the picture again.

"It gives the room a glow," Lavender said. "Lights up the place." It sometimes irritated him in the old office when the lights came on in the afternoon in the shops opposite, especially the neon lights, that they made the old man jumpy as if he were on the razzle. "It made him look tired," he added.

"He'll be quieter in here," said Eeles.

Lavender smiled defensively. If a client came to the place and cracked a joke, such as "It must have been years since the old boy saw his fly," Lavender would close his eyes, offended. A man, Eeles understood, could call his ancestors bastards if he liked, but strangers ought to keep their mouths shut; but he did venture a small joke. "Pity he can't answer the phone."

He and Lavender were usually out on their calls half the day.

"Yes," said Lavender with a short laugh, "it would save me quite a bit on the answering service." Then he became serious and intimate. When he got back from Brussels, Frankfurt or Belfast, he said, "I always drop in here to look at him before I go on to the club. I don't know why."

"Well," said Eeles at last, "I suppose I'd better get home to the wife and kids."

"Yes," said Lavender. "Thanks for coming. You won't have a quick one round the corner?"

Eeles excused himself and Lavender said, looking doggish, "D'you really mean that?"

"Yes," said Eeles.

"Pity," said Lavender. "Oh well—gin and women, always my trouble, as the fellow said."

Two months after the move, Lavender went on business to Hamburg and when he got back Eeles said, "There's a letter from the bank."

"Damn impudence," said Lavender when he read it. "They're all the same, afraid of Head Office. I'll go round in the morning. I'll tell him where he gets off."

Eeles gaped. "He's rung up three times. What are you going to say?" Eeles asked.

"Chop, chop, move the account," said Lavender.

That is what Eeles admired: Lavender's nerve.

"Anything else?"

"Mrs. Baum rang," said Eeles.

After Eeles left that evening and when Lavender was unpacking his samples, a soft but mannish voice called from the door of the outer room. Lavender was raking up an old row he had had with his father and for the moment thought it must be he, although he had died years before. Then he recognized the voice of Mrs. Baum (Prunella Gowns. Wholesale Only). He had been as nervous of a visit from her as he used to be of his father when he was a boy. She was an old business friend and he had not told her that he had moved the office.

"B," she said—he hated to be called Bertrand: hell at school, "effing B-B-Burlington Bertie" when he was in the Navy. Bloody sissy name, weak.

"Those stairs, B! Eeles told me you'd moved."

She opened her fur coat to get her breath back. Her face looked wolfish in a good-natured way and made her look older than she was, but her eyes were dark and alive and sparkled like her rings.

"Sit down, sit down, I'll take your coat," said Lavender.

"I'll keep it," she said.

She was very much a woman, but her voice brought the pleasant chords of men's voices to Lavender's head—Eeles, for example, old Hauser, Alfie, her husband—a long procession going back to "displeasure" Stamford of *Ripper;* and Law who "opened his heart" to him when they were in the hospital in Bombay; Monnier in Saigon; Jack Gibbs; Porter the racing driver who had lost a leg and who had secretly taught him to drive when he was sixteen, which had led to that god-awful row with his father—all worshipped and worshipping. So that when Alfie Baum turned out to be a swine and left Jess Baum for a model at a trade show in Manchester and "broke Jess's heart," she took Alfie's place in the male procession. Lavender felt like marrying her himself in a kind of way; the difficulty was that by that time he was already married to Phyllis, whom Alfie and Jess, as worshippers, had warned him against.

"How is Eeles getting on?" said Mrs. Baum.

"Hard-working. Loyal. Straight as a die," said Lavender.

"What did I tell you?" she said possessively. "If you had listened to me, you would have got rid of Cook years ago."

"Mauvais type," said Lavender. Mrs. Baum made him feel Continental.

She ignored this and looked shrewdly at the bleak office. "Who on earth's that?" she said, pointing to the picture.

"You've seen it before," he said.

"Never."

"Never? That's funny. It was in the old office. G-Great-Uncle Gibbs," said Lavender.

"What's it doing here?"

"Phyllis won't have it in the house; her sister doesn't like it."

Lavender gave the twist to his neck. For him the picture was the great test: by their response to it one knew who saw life as one saw it oneself. Neither Phyllis nor her sister did.

Mrs. Baum sighed. Alfie had told the young Lavender, "Never marry a girl from the same office; as bad as the girl next door."

Then her eyes looked greedy and her face softened. "You'd have to pay a fortune for a frame like that, B. It's Victorian. They don't even make them now. All that goldwork in it," she said. "You can see," she added, "it's a likeness. You told me about him, I know, but I never *pictured* him."

A whole group of fat commercial men, bursting at the waist, came into her suddenly affectionate mind—Alfie, of course; then a cousin of his who was a theatrical agent; and on her side of the family, men whose knees she had sat on when she was a child. Her feelings were for the comforts and the sadness of the flesh. She was on the stout side herself.

"I don't see any of you in him," she said. "Not your figure, not your eyes. Not your father's side of the family. I don't see any Lavender in him, B."

"Best judge of claret south of the Wash," said Lavender. "Left his money to the Lords' Day Observance Society." And added, "Gin and women, always my trouble. Negative father."

Mrs. Baum nodded. Baffled by this word the first time she had heard Lavender use it, she was proud now of knowing the code. Alfie had told her that it came from the days when ships used flag signals and ran up a flag with a X on it to signal: "Cancel last message."

"Not your father's side. Your mother's, I suppose."

"N-no, no, no, no," said Lavender softly as if conjuring up spirits. "Frankly," he said. "Sort of. Let me see, grandmother's, sister's husband—what have you?"

Mrs. Baum was a hard-headed woman but she loved his "No. No. No. No's"; they enveloped him in a mist. The vagueness of Lavender had always attracted her—she seemed to glide with him towards the unknowable. A wave of comforting madness washed over her; her rings sparkled with sentiments and her lips loosened with appetite. She remembered large foggy photographs (but cocoa-colored) in her home as a girl, and people looking silly in colored snaps, but there was nothing as bold, bright, "as large as life and twice as natural," as her mother used to say, like a portrait framed in gold. Her heart —as she grew up—worshipped the sight of old men, pink as babies. They made her feel younger.

"You shouldn't keep a valuable picture like that here," she said restlessly. "Any burglar would lift it for the frame alone."

"Phyllis hates it," he said.

"How is Phyllis?" she asked, without interest.

"Comme ci, comme ça," said Lavender. *"Plus ça change . . ."*

She liked his bits of French. They made her think she had just come back from Paris. As Alfie used to say, he ought to have been on the stage.

"No," added Lavender, and to get off the subject of his wife he changed his face and manner. He became "One"—she always admired that. Not only he, but his truly beautiful suits, seemed to be speaking. "One gets off the boat train late at night, after a couple of double gins, drops the luggage in at the office. There he is, waiting," he said. He waved a hand towards the picture. "The longer one lives, the more one values someone to come back to."

Mrs. Baum felt a short ugly stab in the heart. She knew what he felt. Often she would leave her flat, she said, and go back to the showroom in the evening when the girls had gone and it was closed. "And yet, B, you never *knew* him. I mean, he was dead before you were born. Life is funny the way it takes you . . ." She gazed at the portrait.

"There is more in life than one thinks," said Lavender.

"You're right, B," said Mrs. Baum. "A picture like that can take you back."

"Frankly," he said. "Yes and no."

But Mrs. Baum understood this. In her businesslike way she thought that her life had begun when she was a very young woman and she really did look lovely: you knew it wouldn't last and you packed all you could into it—but men were different. A man like B —like Alfie, too—never got beyond the time when they were boys and, damn them, it kept them young. It came to her as a revelation. B did not see Gibbs when he looked at the picture: he was seeing his childhood.

This was the boring side of men and the damn thing was that they played on your feelings; she could feel this happening to her now. She kept quiet about this and changed the subject.

"How's business?" said Mrs. Baum. "I'll tell you what I came about. My niece, Zita, is getting married, and of all things, she wants to get married in Irish lace . . . I thought I'd pop round to see if you had any."

"Foolish virgin," said Lavender. "Come in here." And she followed him into the outer room. "There you are." And he pointed to the long rolls packed in oiled paper stacked against the walls. "Take your pick. As the American said, 'Brother, you want lace, we've got it.'" And he dropped into his Irish turn as he looked at the labels and tried to lift the top parcel off. "We're on strike, God help us, don't mind the broken windows but t'anks to the Blessed Virgin there's a darling piece for the dear child, me brother won't put a bomb under the place till after the wedding."

Lavender tried to lift one more of the parcels.

Mrs. Baum looked about the room. It was small, and stacks of samples rose halfway up to the window, so that there was scarcely any light. Against one wall there was a small typing desk and a chair.

"Look at that," she said sentimentally, "I had one like that when Alfie and I started up."

The table, he said, was for a German secretary he sometimes had, one of the *haben Sie?*'s.

"Don't bother now," she said.

"There's yards of it here, I know," said Lavender, looking at the dust on his hands. "Eeles has been in Belfast. I'll get him to find some."

"Yes," she said. "Don't spoil that beautiful suit. Look at your hands. Let's go and have a drink."

"Will do," he said, relieved. "This stuff weighs a ton, it gets you in the back. I'll wash this off."

She liked the distress he showed when he looked at his blackened hands. He went to wash them in an alcove in his own office, and while she waited she went up to the portrait of Great-Uncle Gibbs and put a finger out and touched it. Lavender returned, and seeing her near the picture, straightened it and then put his blotter straight on his desk, saw that the telephone books were in the right order on Eeles's table. Then he got his coat from the coat stand, remarking that Eeles had only one bad habit: he often used Lavender's peg by mistake.

"Small things," he said, "irritate."

Mrs. Baum liked a man who fussed about small things. Alfie had fussed about his shirts.

Lavender gave one last look at the picture before they left. "You can call it sentimental or what you like, but if I was down to my last penny, I wouldn't sell Great-Uncle Gibbs."

"What's wrong with sentiment?" she said, taking his arm. He looked up and they walked to the stairs of the silent, empty building.

"Let's go to Giuseppe's."

Giuseppe's was a bar in a large hotel a hundred yards around the corner, and still holding his arm, Mrs. Baum felt what she always liked about Lavender. Cook had called him a snob and a fool, Alfie had told him to grow up, but Lavender was a gentleman who took your mind off things: he was like a whole crowd of men, yet blessed with a loneliness like her own. The street outside was empty at this time of the evening except for an occasional couple like themselves. Their footsteps echoed off the walls of the closed offices and the windows of closed sandwich bars, and were suddenly silent as they passed an empty, gravelike doorway.

They found themselves on the huge carpet of the hotel on which thousands of pairs of shoes without people in them might be tread-

ing. The place was empty now but notable for packed trade shows
where she and Alfie and B had often met. The lounge immediately
inside was remarkable for a row of tall bronze dancers standing on
marble pillars and each holding a tray or a brass tambourine over her
head, presumably to cheer the models who arrived. Mrs. Baum
remembered sitting at a table there and Alfie telling her to give up
her job in Birmingham and start up in his business with him; she
had often mentioned this to Lavender. They went past this now
empty hall, done in what Alfie had said was in the Moorish style,
into the enormous paneled bar, also empty, where the barman was
reading a paper.

"*Il ne marche pas,*" said Lavender.

"It's dead," she said. "No trade since Giuseppe left."

"Negative Giuseppe," said Lavender, swinging her back to the
doors.

"Let's go round to the flat," she said scornfully to the empty bar.

"Hard to starboard," he said, leading her out.

They arrived at her block of flats, built in white tiles suited to
plumbing on a vast scale. He knew the place well.

There was always something wrong in his cottage in the country
when he got home on Saturday mornings. "Poor Phyllis," he said,
always would put his piles of *Punch* in the wrong order, and never
learned to draw a pair of curtains properly, and never put things away
in the kitchen. After the Navy it drove him mad. She had a peculiar
habit of standing behind him when he was reading which he could
not cure her of, and it brought on the pain in his back because it
reminded him of the time when Flo Gibbs, the sister of the superb
Jack—much older than himself—whom he had worshipped, had
pushed him off the tree. He ought to have married Flo but she was
much too rich, or one of dear old Hauser's Swiss daughters, any one
of them. They could run a house and old Hauser would have been
in and out. He would have had a son whom he could have put into
the Navy. A man's life, not like the rag trade.

Mrs. Baum's three rooms, kitchen and bathroom were spotless
and would have passed an admiral's inspection. He liked the white
curtains with their large tomatolike spots, the spongy leather sofa
that slumped like the perfect substitute for Alfie in the room, sug-

gesting that Mrs. Baum had no intention, indeed no need of marrying again. He liked that: an ideal. He liked its rival, the blue, yellow and white Chinese carpet, although the glass-topped dining table upset him. Sitting at it, one could see other people's feet. The place was so much fresher than it had been in Alfie's cigar-smoking time.

How often he and Mrs. Baum had sat there talking of this and that! The sofa was made for going over the past.

"You go and get the drinks, B," called Mrs. Baum from her bedroom. "You know where they are."

"Gin and women . . ." Lavender began. And when she came back and as they raised their glasses, he said, "Happy nights."   "And no regrets," she said.

"So you're flying to Frankfurt again," she said.

"Negative aircraft," he said. "By sea."

She knew that, of course.

"No," he said and told her what he had told her a dozen times before. She liked her flat to have someone else's voice saying the same things again and again.

"No," he said, holding up his hand and closing his eyes for a second or two, so that his blank eyelids made him look as if he were going into a trance and that he was telling her not to interrupt him in a sacred matter. "When Jack Gibbs retired he took a house in France for the winter and he always got a cabin on one of the *Queens* as far as Cherbourg. 'Only way to travel: see the Channel.' Jack was right. I always go via Cherbourg.

"Last time I went an American said to me," Lavender went on, " 'Brother, if you're heading for Frankfurt, you're on the wrong ship.' 'Saves time', I said and told him. 'Well, I'll be darned,' he said.

"No," said Lavender, defying reason in a way that gave Mrs. Baum one more twinge of worship. "One picks up the *Queen* at Southampton. Go straight to old Frank at the bar, pink gin, double of course. 'Nice to see you again, sir. Blowy tonight.' 'Glad to hear it.' 'Bad for the bar, sir.' 'Only thing I miss, she doesn't roll. *Ripper* bucked like a horse. One misses that.' 'Not me, sir, I was in minesweepers.' A few more double gins and in six hours one is at Cherbourg, wakey, wakey, Paris train waiting for you, cut across Paris in time for a bottle of Chablis at the Café de la Paix. *'La sole*

meunière comme toujours, Monsieur Lavandaire,' to the Gare de
l'Est and you're in Frankfurt eleven o'clock. *Haben Sie?*'s all round
you. It's the only way. One can argue that it takes longer and costs
more . . ."

"Well, B, it does," said Mrs. Baum. "It only takes an hour by air."

"But people *know* one," said Lavender, shutting his eyes again.
"You know where you are. Dear old Hauser, he wouldn't fly either.
I was thinking of him. Swiss have no navy. Had to take the train from
Zürich, but crossed Dover-Calais. Kept him young. And . . ."

"Help yourself to another," said Mrs. Baum. "Nothing for me."

"Great-Uncle Gibbs always took the boat to Copenhagen or the
Hook even when he was turned eighty," said Lavender, pouring
himself a drink.

"Flying hadn't been invented. Alfie was never near a boat in his
life," said Mrs. Baum.

"That's what was wrong with him," said Lavender.

Mrs. Baum switched on the television. "Oh dear," she said. "Look
at that. Another bomb in Belfast. I hope Eeles is all right."

She switched it off. "I can't stand it," she said. "You get your shop
burned down—what for?"

"Eeles?" said Lavender, looking at his watch. "He's on his way
back by now. Nothing can touch Eeles anyway.

"No," he went on. "Up and down the Channel, bringing in a
convoy at night with the fireworks going—Alfie would have enjoyed
it. I think of it when I go to Cherbourg. One goes on deck and a
flash of summer lightning brings it back, the sea lit up like an ice
rink and some silly sod says 'Where's the cat?' when the stuff comes
over. Cat hated gunfire. Sunrise, all quiet, and the cat comes back
and the signal comes through: 'Thank you, *Ripper*, rather a nice
party, I think.' Stamford was always sloshed to the eyeballs when he
went up to the bridge at Dover, stone sober when he got outside."

Mrs. Baum had heard this story very often and said pleasantly,
"Alfie always took our accounts down to the shelter in the war if
anything happened. We moved the office to Bury St. Edmunds.
Wasn't that near your uncle's place?"

"Bury . . ." Lavender began, but stopped because the telephone
rang.

Mrs. Baum answered it. "Who?" said Mrs. Baum. "No. I can't. I have people here." And banged down the telephone in a sudden temper.

"What's that?" said Lavender.

"That's the trouble with this place, B," she said. "It's not what it was. They've let a different class of people in, you don't know who they are. When you're on your own you feel nervous. I never used to feel like that. It is a man called Williams on the tenth floor. He keeps pestering me. He knocked on the door three nights ago. I keep the chain on now."

Lavender tried to rise from the sofa. "What's his number? I'll tell him where to get off," he said and knocked his glass over.

"Stay where you are," said Mrs. Baum. "Don't move till I get a cloth."

"On your carpet," said Lavender, getting up at last and following her, and when she came out of the kitchen he tried to pull the cloth from her.

"I'll do it," she said. And got down on her knees and rubbed.

Lavender admired this. She was stout but looked very neat on her knees and her hair kept its shape. When she stood up, Lavender took the cloth from her and went down on his knees too and continued to rub. He even moved the sofa in case any of the drink had gone under it. "Careful of your back," Mrs. Baum said. "Don't spoil your suit."

"Negative suit," he said.

She fetched a clothes brush. She was impressed by his brushing: a fastidious man.

"Give yourself another drink," she said.

Lavender got himself another large one and stood it carefully on the table, but did not drink. It stood there, still as an idol.

Her friendly voice suddenly had a note of accusation. "I rang the club the other day and they said you weren't living there any more."

Lavender's talking face became still and he stared at her a long time and then his voice took on the general, indignant noise of men grumbling at a bar. "The food's gone off. Usual story. New chef. They put the prices up."

"You resigned?" she said, shocked and insinuating.

"Yes and no. Sort of."

He looked ashamed.

He had taken her to dinner there more than once on Ladies' Night. He must be doing well to belong to a club like this, she thought. Paintings of inhumanly tall field marshals, admirals, viceroys in splendid frames and with killing eyes, hung in the vast Dining Room. The effect of all this glorious manliness was girlish. It was like a dress show for men, a sunrise of hermaphrodites—it excited her. She admired especially the sapphire sash which one of those eminences was wearing across his breast—not this season's color for women, too pale—but she found herself thinking more than once that a sash like that would have suited Lavender and that she could easily get one of the girls in the workroom to make him one. Blue, she had daydreamed, was the color of Uncle Gibbs's eyes—*Great*-Uncle Gibbs, why did she always make that mistake and call him Uncle?

She always put on something fashionable, not in the shops yet, but in spite of the imperial splash on the walls, most of the tables were empty—only a few old people were there and the women looked proud of being dowdy in their biscuit-colored cardigans. The room was cold and the waiters were negligent; all foreigners, she supposed, who couldn't understand Lavender's English. They fetched one who was baffled by his French. "All *haben Sie?*'s," he said. The good thing was the sight of Lavender blinking at the wine list as if it were sacred and then hearing him say, "Châteauneuf-du-Pape—old Hauser drank nothing else." But Gibbs was a claret man. So was Jack.

Now as they sat on the sofa in her flat, she said, "They want to put my rent up. I haven't made up my mind. What were we talking about when that prowler Williams rang?"

For it struck her that Lavender was not touching his drink: giving up his room at the club, moving into a pokey office at the back of the building. Something wrong?

"Drink up," she said gently. He drank.

"Bury, that was it," he said. "You mentioned Bury."

"When Alfie and I were in Bury we drove out to a posh hotel in the country, with long crinkly chimneys. On a hill," she said.

"Nor'west of Bury?" Lavender asked.

"I never know which is south, east or west," she said, laughing. "The name will come to me . . ."

Lavender ran off a list of small towns and villages: Flaxton, Pyke Market, Market Plympton, Bush Vale, Lord Beverley's place with the long grey wall which Lavender had climbed over to see the deer when he was a boy.

"Something Manor," she said. "Littlestone?" she said.

"Lytestone," he corrected her.

He slipped into his tragic Saint Bernard look: his youthfulness vanished and he put his hand over his forehead.

"Don't go on," he said. "The Gibbs place."

"That's what Alfie said. We had a lovely room," she said, leading him on. (With all that Gibbs money behind him, why did he resign from the club?) "With a balcony. The car park was packed. People coming and going all night. They couldn't complain of business. Fancy that belonging to your uncle. We wondered which room you had when you lived there. We were talking about you."

Lavender watched the red spots on Mrs. Baum's curtains arrange themselves in vertical lines and begin to move upwards, reach the rail and descend in a shower and then slowly move up again.

"*Great-*uncle," Lavender corrected her. "What room?"

"When you stayed; when you visited."

He stared at her. The red tomatolike spots on the curtain began to rise faster like a reel unwinding.

"When you were a boy," she said.

Lavender stared at Mrs. Baum and his reddened face turned as pale as veined stone. His stare was concentrated, and if a minute before he was drunkish, he was now sober. He was accusing her, examining her, suspecting her, searching her with an intensity that made her uncomfortable. He waved a hand, waving her away, but she was still there. She wished she had not spoken.

"My room?" he said.

"Yes," she teased. "I bet they put you next door to your cousin Jack."

"Flo," he said sharply.

"Flo," she said. "I knew it. The one who pushed you off the tree.

I can see it all. You've been a lucky devil, B. Fancy being brought
up in that lovely place. The staircase! There was an old gardener who
had been there when the family had it. You'd know him. He showed
us round the garden. Have you ever been back? You ought to do
that. It's interesting."

Lavender looked away from her, but he put out his hand and
gripped her by the wrist. His hand was large and strong and hurt her.

"What was the gardener's name?" he said.

"I don't remember—but he said he remembered you."

"He's a bloody liar," he said.

"You're hurting me, B. That's what he said. You ought to go and
see it—you ought to see where I was brought up, Stepney! Alfie and
I had to laugh. Well, the servants they must have had to run a place
like that! We asked which room you had."

He let go of her hand and turned to face her. He said in a jeering
voice, hurrying over the words, "Over the stables at the back. Sixteen
months, Mother's cousin was cook there. I was ten."

"You never told me that, B," said Mrs. Baum, who loved exciting
news. "Alfie and I thought you were brought up there."

"A fellow called Law, the best friend a man ever had, when we
were in hospital in Bombay, he opened his heart to me. He came
from Stepney. I told him. His mother was a cook. We used to go
for walks and talk of this and that, private things," he said, shutting
his eyes.

"Well," said Mrs. Baum taking a big breath. "We've come a long
way, B. I wasn't prying into your private affairs."

He got up and got himself another drink.

"You know your trouble, B. You've got a soft heart," she said.

"No, no, no, no, no," he said, cheering up as he created what she
called his mist. And suddenly he said loudly, "Lytestone taught me
something. I made a vow . . ."

But the red tomatolike spots of the curtains started once more to
stream upwards and he lost what he was going to say. He had a
confused feeling that she might be Law. He wanted to tell her things
he had told Law, but all he could remember was Jack Gibbs's
playroom with a whole fleet of little lead models of ships set out on
the floor. Not to be moved unless Jack said so, and he was older.

Battle of Jutland. Then Jack letting him move one ship, then two, shouting to his sister Flo to clear out. That was why she pushed him off the tree, bang on his back, afterwards. Unconscious. Doctor. That's why they had to let him stay all that time.

He struggled to explain this to Mrs. Baum (or was she Law?), that he worshipped Jack, as he tried to stop them becoming spots on the curtains. Only one thing was certain: "Chop, chop," he said. "All gone. House sold. Auction."

"B," she said. "Sit down. I'll get us some coffee."

"Wait," he commanded. "I bought the picture. Fifty pence. Damn shame. No one left in the family would touch it," he said.

She was hurrying to the kitchen.

"Negative coffee," he shouted to her. "I made a vow . . ."

She looked back. "I can hear, B," she said.

"To look after the poor old bastard," he muttered to himself. He got up and made a wild swing towards the bottles and then wheeled back and flopped onto the sofa, astonished. She turned off the stove, but by the time she got to him he had passed out.

For a while she considered him. Once he seemed to speak.

"Gin and women. Chop. Chop," he said.

She waited anxiously, but he said nothing else. She cautiously got a chair and put it near his feet and she lifted them on it. She opened the door to the bathroom and was in and out of the kitchen, eating a bun, watching him. His breathing became louder. There was a kind of happiness in seeing him there. It was like having Alfie back. After two hours she understood he was there for the night. She took off his shoes and got a rug to put over him. She turned down all lights except one, went to her own room and left her door ajar in case he stirred. For the first time since Alfie left her she felt safe for the night and slept deeply.

In the morning she heard him in the bathroom. She put on one of her gaudier dressing gowns and came in when he was dressed. He looked heavy in the face and flinched at the brilliant red-and-yellow garment, but said, "Very sorry about last night. Something went wrong with the steering. Did I say anything?"

"That's all right—you never stopped," she said, laughing.

He had folded the blanket neatly, straightened the sofa.

"Feeling better?"

She brought him a cup of coffee.

"Now," she said firmly, "When did you give up the club?"

"Two months ago," he said.

"I don't mean that," she said. "Where have you been staying? At the cottage?"

"No, no, no, no, no," he said quickly. "Fares have gone up. Negative cottage."

"Where, B? With your sister?"

"Yes and no," he said. "At the office."

"What!" she shouted.

"I've got a sleeping bag. By the way, don't tell Eeles. I put it away every morning before he comes. I walk up the street. Turn round. He's always there on time."

"On the floor—with your back? What is wrong?" she said. "Is it Eeles?"

Mrs. Baum was perplexed by him and by herself: there was an expression of disaster concealed in Lavender's face which made her feel masterly and grand. She was prosperous: energy had flowed out of her after Alfie had left her, but she missed the sense of gamble that always seemed to hang about Alfie. It struck her as being rather fine that B had rescued the picture of that ugly old man who was no connection of his—it was silly but it showed a sort of decency —and that his mother's cousin had been a cook in that house.

"You haven't sacked Eeles, have you?" she said suspiciously.

"No," said Lavender. "He's been in Ireland settling the strike."

Well, she thought, that's not what's on his mind. "Has he settled it?"

"Yes and no. It settled itself. Depends which way you look at it. They pinched the looms out of the factory and two of the machines and put a bomb in it. Negative workshop. Bloody funny really. They're all on social security—except Eeles and me."

"Why didn't you tell me last night?" she said to him. "Was Eeles all right?"

"Oh yes," said Lavender. "Sergeant, ex-armored cars. Straight as a die. You're all right there. You walk down the middle of the street with a bottle of whisky sticking out of your coat pocket. Like going up the Yangtze in the war—we always kept to the middle of the river. By the way, he'll have got the lace. He probably went round to the fellow who pinched it."

"Well, thank you, but I can't spend the morning talking about the Yangtze," Mrs. Baum said. "I've got to get to the showroom. When are you coming back from Frankfurt? None of this Cherbourg nonsense: take the plane. Cook left you holding the baby with that Irish business. You've lost a lot of money. Stick to Frankfurt. When are you coming back? Wednesday? Are you going home?"

"No, no, no, no, no," said Lavender. "Negative home."

That "negative" shocked her, but she shook off her pain.

"I sometimes feel sorry for your wife, B," she said. "But you can't sleep on the floor in that office. I won't have it. You'd better come here. That will keep Williams quiet. And we've got to have a talk. You've got to cut down your expenses."

They left the flats. The commissionaire gave a sort of salute and Mrs. Baum held her chin up and looked very grand and very respectable. They parted at the street corner.

"What did you pay at the club?" she asked.

"One way and another, if you reckon it up—" he began.

"Tell me on Wednesday," she said. "You could bring Great-Uncle Gibbs." And at that afterthought she sighed. It was the wrong thing to say.

"I don't think Eeles would like that," he said sternly.

"Anyway . . ." she said and went away, saying to herself, "I'm a fool."

Outside the office Eeles was reading his paper, and though surprised to see Lavender coming up the street instead of coming down it, he followed him up the stairs into the office.

THE
VICE-CONSUL

U nder the blades of the wide fan turning slowly in its Yes-No tropical way, the vice-consul sloped in his office, a soft and fat man, pink as a ham, the only pink man in the town, and pimpled by sweat. He was waiting for the sun to go down into the clouds over the far bank of the estuary, ten miles wide here, and to put an end to a bad week. He had been plagued by the officers and crew of a Liverpool ship, the *Ivanhoe*, smoking below in the harbor. There was trouble about shipping a puma.

His Indian clerk put his head in at the door and said in the whisper of the tropics, "Mr. McDowell's here."

Years at this post on the river had reduced the vice-consul's voice also to the same sort of whisper, but he had a hoarseness that gave it rank. He believed in flying off the handle and showing authority by using allusions which his clerk could not understand.

"Not the bloody Twenty-third Psalm from that blasted tramp again," he said and was glad McDowell heard it as he pushed in earnestly after the clerk. McDowell was a long-legged man with an unreasonable chin and emotional knees.

"I've brought Felden's license," he said.

"I ought to have had it a week ago," said the vice-consul. "Have you got the animal aboard yet? It was on the dock moaning away all day. You could hear it up here."

"We've got it on deck," said McDowell.

"Typical hunter," said the vice-consul, "thinking he could ship it without a license. They've no feeling for animals and they're liars too."

"No hearts," said McDowell.

At this low hour at the end of the day, the vice-consul did not care to have a ship's officer trump his own feelings.

It was part of the vice-consul's martyrdom during his eight years at the port that he was, so to say, the human terminus on whom hunters, traders, oilmen, television crews, sailors whose minds had been inflated by dealing with too much geography, dumped their boasts. Nature in the shape of thousands of miles of jungle, flat as kale, thousands of miles of river, tributaries, drifting islands of forest rubbish, not to mention millions of animals, snakes, bloodsucking fish, swarms of migrating birds, butterflies and biting insects, had scared them and brought them down to the river to unload their fantasies.

"Take your boa constrictor . . ." they began. "Take your alligator . . . Take your marching ant . . ."

Now he had to "take" a man called Felden who had tried to stuff him up with the tale that his fourteen-year-old son had caught the beast on his fishing line in a backwater above Manaos.

The vice-consul was a sedentary man and longed to hear a fact. "When do you sail?" he said when McDowell sat down on an upright chair which was too small for him.

"The day after tomorrow," said McDowell.

"I can't say I'll be sorry to see you lot go," said the vice-consul, making his usual speech to departing sailors. "I'd like to know where the hell your company gets its crews."

"I'm from Belfast," said McDowell, placing his hands on those knees.

"Oh, nothing personal," said the vice-consul. He stamped the license, pushed it across his desk and stood up, but McDowell did not move. He leaned forward and said, "Would you do me a favor?"

"What favor?" said the vice-consul, offended.

McDowell started to caress his knees as if to get their help. "Would you be able to recommend a dentist in the town?" he said.

The vice-consul sat down, made a space on his desk and said, "Well, that's a change. I thought you were going to tell me you had got yourself clapped like the rest of your crew and wanted a doctor. Dentist? Afraid not. There isn't a dentist in the place, not one I'd recommend, anyway. You've been here three weeks and can see for yourself. Half the population have no teeth at all. None of the women, anyway. Go down the street, and if you're not careful, you can walk straight down their throats."

McDowell nodded. The vice-consul wanted more than a nod.

"It stands to reason," he said, expanding. "What do they get to eat? Dried meat and manioc covered in bird droppings, fish that tastes of newspaper from the bloody river. No fresh milk, no fresh meat, no fresh vegetables—everything has to be flown in and they can't afford it. It would kill them if they could."

McDowell shook his head and kept his knees still. "Catholic country," he said.

"No topsoil," said the vice-consul, putting on a swagger. "If you've got a pain in the jaw, I'm sorry. Take my advice and do what I do. Get on the next plane to Miami. Or Puerto Rico if you like. It'll cost you a penny or two but it's the only way. Sorry for you. Painful."

"Oh," said McDowell, sitting back like an idol. "My teeth are all right," he said.

"Then what do you want a dentist for?"

"It's my dentures," McDowell said, gleaming as he made the distinction.

"All right—dentures," said the vice-consul.

"They've gone. Stolen."

The vice-consul looked at McDowell for a long time. The jaws did not move, so he turned sideways and now studied McDowell, screwing up one annoyed eye. The man swallowed.

"Mr. McDowell," he said, taking the syllables one by one. "Are you feeling the heat? Just give your mouth a tap. If I'm not mistaken, you're wearing them."

McDowell let his arms fall to his sides and parted his lips: a set of teeth gleamed as white and righteous as a conjuring trick. "I never sail without me spares," he said.

The vice-consul wasn't going to stand funny business from British subjects. He had an air for this.

"Very wise," he said. "You fellows are always getting your teeth knocked out by your pals. Makes you careful, I suppose. What do you want *me* to do? You've got a captain, haven't you?" He became suspicious. "I suppose you're not thinking of Filing an Official Complaint," he said, pulling a form out of his drawer, waving it at McDowell and putting it back, "because I can tell you, officially, that who pinches what from whom on the bloody *Ivanhoe* is no concern of mine, unless it's connected with mutiny, wounding, murder or running guns."

The vice-consul knew this kind of speech by heart.

The sun had floundered down into the clouds; he shouted to his clerk to put on the light but switched it on himself. He decided to match McDowell on the meaning of words.

"You said 'stole,' McDowell. You must have some prize thieves in your crew. But will you tell me how you get a set of dentures out of a man's head against his will, even when he's asleep, unless he's drugged or tied up. Were you drunk?"

"I've never touched a drop in my life," said McDowell.

"I suppose not," said the vice-consul coldly.

"I took them out myself. I always put my dentures in a glass."

"So I should hope," said the vice-consul. "Filthy leaving them in. Dangerous too. What else did they take? Watch? Wallet? Glasses?"

McDowell spoke carefully, picking over the peculiarity of an austere and personal case. "Only my dentures," he said. "It wasn't the crew. I don't mix with them. They read magazines. They never think. I wasn't aboard," he said softly, adding to his mystery. "It wasn't at night. I was ashore. In the afternoon. Off duty."

The Indian clerk put his head in at the door and looked anxiously from McDowell to the vice-consul.

"What do you want now? Can't you see I'm busy?" said the vice-consul.

The man's head disappeared and he shut the door.

McDowell stretched his long arms and placed his hands on his knees and his fingers began to drag at his trousers. "I saw it with my own eyes," he said. "I saw this girl with them. When the rain started."

"What girl?" the vice-consul said, lighting a cigar and putting a haze of smoke between himself and his torment. "The rainy season started six weeks ago," he swaggered. "You get your thunderstorm every afternoon. They come in from the west and build up over the river at two o'clock to the minute and last till ten past three. You can set your watch by them."

The vice-consul owned the climate.

"Tropical rain," he said grandly, "not the drizzle you get in Belfast. The rain comes down hot, straight out of the kettle, floods the streets and dries up in ten minutes, not a sign of it except the damn trees grow a foot higher. The trouble is that it doesn't clear the air: the heat is worse afterwards. You feel you're breathing—I don't know—boiled stair carpet my wife says, but that's by the way. He waved at the smoke. "You'll tear the knees of those trousers of yours if you don't leave them alone."

A dressy man, he pointed his cigar at them. McDowell's knees stuck out so far that the vice-consul, who was a suspicious man, felt that they were making a displeasing personal claim on him. They indeed gave a jump when McDowell shouted in a voice that had the excitement of sudden fever, "I can stand thunder. But I can't stand lightning, sheet or forked. It brings my dinner up. It gets under your armpits. A gasometer went up in Liverpool when I was a boy and was blown blazing across the Mersey—"

"I thought you said you came from Belfast," said the vice-consul. "Lightning never bothers me."

"There was this thunderbolt," said McDowell, ignoring him and his voice went to a whisper. "I'm in the entrance of this hotel, looking at the alligator handbags to take one home for my wife and I've just picked one up and down comes this bolt, screaming behind my back, with a horrible violet flame, and sends me flying headfirst up the passage. There's a girl there, polishing the floor, and all the lights go out. The next thing, I'm in an open doorway, I'm pitching headfirst onto a bed in the room and I get my head under the clothes. It's like the end of the world and I'm praying into the pillow. I think I am dead, don't I?"

"I don't know," said the vice-consul coldly. "But what do you do at sea? And where was this place?"

"It's natural at sea," said McDowell, calming down. "The Columbus. Yes, it would be the Columbus."

"Never heard of it," said the vice-consul.

"I don't know how long I am there, but when it gets quieter I look up, the lightning is going on and off in the window and that's when I see this girl standing by the mirror—"

"The one who was polishing the floor, I suppose," said the vice-consul with contentment.

"No," said McDowell, "this one was in the bed when I fell on it, on top of her, I told you."

"You didn't. You pulled her in," said the vice-consul.

McDowell stopped, astonished, but went on, "Standing by the mirror, without a stitch of clothing on her. Terrible. She takes my dentures out of the glass, and the next thing, she opens her mouth wide and she's trying to fit them, this way and that, to her poor empty gums."

"You couldn't see all that in a flash of lightning. You must have switched the light on," said the vice-consul.

McDowell slapped his knee and sat back in a trance of relief. "You're right," he said gratefully. "Thank God you reminded me. I wouldn't want to tell a lie. The sight of her with her poor empty mouth destroyed me. I'll never forget it. It'd break a man's heart."

"Not mine," said the vice-consul. "It's disgusting. Shows ignorance too. No two human jawbones are alike."

"The pitiful ignorance, you're right!" said McDowell. "I called out to her, 'Careful what you're doing! You might swallow them. Put them back in the glass and come back to bed.'"

The tropical hoarseness left the vice-consul's voice. "Ah," he shouted and put his cigar down. "I thought we'd come to it. In plain English, you had come ashore to commit fornication."

"I did not," said McDowell, shocked. "Her sister works for the airline."

"Oh, it's no business of mine. I don't care what you do, but you were in bed with that girl. You said so yourself. But why in God's name did you take your dentures out? In the middle of the afternoon?"

McDowell was even more shocked. He sat back sternly in his chair. "It would have looked hardly decent," he said, "I mean on an *occasion* like that, for any man to keep his teeth in when a poor girl had none of her own. It was politeness. You'd want to show respect. I've got my principles."

He became confident and said, "My dentures have gold clips. Metal attracts lightning—I mean, if you had your mouth open, you might be struck dead. That's another reason why I took them out. You never know who the Lord will strike."

"Both of you, I expect," said the vice-consul.

"Yes," said McDowell, "but you've got to think of others."

The vice-consul got out his handkerchief and wiped his face and his head.

"You'd never get away with this twaddle in a court of law," said the vice-consul. "None of this proves she stole your dentures."

"She had gone when I woke up, and they had gone. The rain was pouring down outside or I would have gone after her," said McDowell.

"And you wouldn't have caught her if you had," said the vice-consul with deep pleasure. "She sold them before she got to the end of the street. You can say goodbye to that lot. You're wasting my time. I've got two other British ships docking in an hour. I've told you what to do. Keep clear of the police. They'll probably arrest you. And if you want a new set of dentures, go to Miami as I said."

"But they're not for *me,* " exclaimed McDowell. "I want them for this girl. I've got the money. It's wrong to steal. Her sister knows it and so does she. If you see a soul in danger, you've got to try and save them.

"God help me," said the vice-consul. "I've got enough trouble in this port as it is, but as a matter of interest, who told you to go to this place—the Columbus—to buy handbags? You can get them at every shop in the town. The river's crawling with alligators."

McDowell nodded to the outer office where the Indian clerk sat. "That gentleman."

"He did, did he?" said the vice-consul, laughing for the first time and achieving a louder shout to his clerk.

The Indian clerk came in. He loved to be called in when the vice-consul was talking business. He gleamed with the prestige of an only assistant. The vice-consul spoke to him in Portuguese with the intimacy of one who sketches his way through a language not his own. The clerk nodded and nodded and talked eagerly.

"My clerk says," said the vice-consul, in his large way, "that you came in at midday the day before yesterday and asked where you could get a girl. He says he knows the airline girl and her sister. He knows the whole family. The father has the barbershop opposite the church and he is a dentist too. He buys up teeth, mostly after funerals."

The clerk nodded and added a few words.

"He says he fixed him up. He says this man's got the biggest collection of teeth in the town."

The clerk's neck was thin; he was like wood. He opened his mouth wide with pride for McDowell to see. There were five sharp steel teeth and two with gold in them.

The vice-consul went on, "He says he often sells them to missionaries. The Dominicans have a mission here. The poor devils come back from far up in the Indian settlements looking like skeletons after three years and with their teeth dropping out. I told you: no calcium. No fresh vegetables. No milk. The climate . . ."

The Indian said no more.

McDowell got up and moved towards the clerk suspiciously, setting his chin. "What's he say about the Dominicans?" said McDowell in a threatening way.

The vice-consul said, "He says you could go down to this man, this barber chap, and you might find your teeth."

The Indian nodded.

"If you don't—well, they've been snapped up and are being flown up the river. Sorry, McDowell, that's all we can do. Take my advice and get back double-quick to your ship. Good day."

The vice-consul picked up some papers and called to McDowell as he left the room, "They'll be up there, preaching The Word."

The following day the vice-consul went out to the *Ivanhoe* to have a last drink with the captain and to have a look at the puma, and grinned when it opened its mouth and snarled at him. The captain said McDowell would be all right once he got to sea, and went on to some tale about a man who claimed to have a cat that backed horses.

It's the bloody great river that does it, the vice-consul thought as he was put ashore afterwards and as he walked home in the dark and saw all the people whispering in their white cotton clothes, looking like ghosts. He was thinking it was only another year before his leave and that he was the only human being in the town.

THE
ACCOMPANIST

It was the afternoon. Joyce had been with me for nearly two hours when suddenly she leaned over me to look at my watch on the table.

"Half past four," she cried in a panic. "Stop it. I shall be late," and scrambling out of bed, she started getting into her clothes in a rush. She frowned when she caught me watching her. I liked watching her dress: her legs and arms were thin, and as she put up her arms to fasten her bra and leaned forward to pull on her tights she seemed to be playing a game of turning herself into comic triangles. She snatched her pale-blue jersey and pulled it over her head, and when her fair hair came out at the top she was saying, "Don't forget. Half past seven. Don't be difficult. You've got to come, William. Bertie will be upset if you don't. Ivy and Jim will be there and Bertie wants you to tell them about Singapore."

In a love affair, one discovers a gift for saying things with two meanings.

"If they are going to be there, Bertie won't miss *me,* " I said. "He used to be mad about Ivy, asked her to marry him once—you told me."

"You are not to say that," Joyce said fiercely as she dragged her jersey down. "Bertie wanted to marry a lot of girls."

So I said yes, I would be there. She put on her coat, which I thought was too thin for a cold day like this, and said, "Look at the time. Hendrick will be so angry," as she struggled away from my long kiss. Her skin burned and there were two red patches on her cheeks. Then she went.

It was only on her "music days" when she was rehearsing with Hendrick that we were able to meet.

Afterwards I went to the window hoping to see her on the street, but I missed her. I pulled a cover over the bed, walked about and then I came across a shopping bag on the table. Joyce had forgotten it. I looked into the bag and saw it contained eight small apple pies packed in cartons: Joyce was a last-minute shopper and they were obviously meant for the dinner we were all going to eat that evening. Well, there was nothing to be done. I could hardly take them to

Bertie's and say, "Your wife left these at my place." Before I left at seven o'clock I ate one. It was cold and dry, but after seeing Joyce, I always felt hungry.

It was a cross-London journey into the decaying district where she and Bertie lived. One had to take one bus, then wait for another. Their flat was on the ground floor of a once respectable Victorian villa. I was glad to arrive at the same time as four other guests, all of us old friends of Bertie's: André, an enormous young Belgian in a fur coat; his toylike wife, Podge; an unmarried girl who adored Bertie and who rarely said anything; and a sharp dark political girl who worked on a review Bertie sometimes wrote for.

Bertie himself came to the door wearing old-fashioned felt slippers. It was odd to see them on a young man who was even younger than we were—not yet thirty. He had a copy of *Le Monde* in his hand and he waved it in the air as he shouted "Well done!" to all of us in the voice of a housemaster at the School Sports. And as we went in he was jubilant, crowing like a cockerel. "My errant spouse," he said, "is at this moment, I presume, toiling across the metropolis and will be here soon. You see, this is one of Joyce's music days. Hendrick's concert is coming on the week after next and he makes her rehearse the whole time, poor wretch. Of course, it's awfully nice for her."

(Bertie loved things to be "awfully nice.")

"He had discovered," Bertie went on proudly, "that she is the only accompanist he can work with. It's very useful, too"—Bertie looked over his glasses sideways at us—"it brings in the pennies. And it gives me time to catch up on *The Times* and *Le Monde.*"

And he slapped the paper against his leg with something like passion. Then he led us into the bedroom where we were to leave our coats.

Except for André, we were all poor in those days. Flats were hard to find. It had taken Bertie and Joyce a long time to find this one —they had had to make do with Bertie's old room—and they had to wait for Bertie's family furniture to arrive out of storage from the North. As we took off our coats we felt the chill of the large room and I understood Joyce's embarrassed giggles when she spoke of it. It was, in the late-Victorian way, high and large; the moldings on the ceiling, a thing now admired, looked like a dusty wedding cake with cracks in it. There was a huge marbled and empty fireplace, but —at variance with the period—brutal red tiles were jammed around it and it was like an enormous empty mouth, hungry for coal or the meals served there when the room had been the dining room of earlier generations. In front of it, without curb or fender, a very small electric fire—not turned on—stood like a modern orphan. Bertie was careful with money, and he and Joyce had not been able to afford to redecorate the room. One could detect small faded flowers in the grey wallpaper; in the bay window hung three sets of curtains: net for privacy, then a lighter greenish summer set, and over them heavy, once banana-colored, curtains, faded at the folds, like the old trailing robes of a dead Edwardian lady.

But it was the enormous bed that, naturally, appalled me. The headboard was of monumental walnut, scrolled at the top, and there were legs murderous to a bare foot. Over the bed was spread a pink satiny coverlet, decorated by love knots and edged by lace from the days of Bertie's parents, even grandparents. It suggested to me a sad Arthurian barge, a washed-out poem from some album of the Love's Garland kind. There was, of course, a dressing table with its many little shelves, and one had the fear of seeing dead heroines in its mirrors and even, in the cold, seeing their breath upon the glass. I caught sight of my own face in it, looking Chinese and sarcastic: I tried to improve my expression. Faded, faded—everything faded. The only human things in the room were our coats thrown on the bed—I dropped mine out of pity on what I hoped was Joyce's side of it—and the hem of one of Joyce's dresses characteristically caught by the doors of a huge wardrobe. The sight of it made me feel the misty air of the room was quivering with Joyce's tempers and her tears.

But I exaggerate—there was one more human thing: Bertie's old desk from his Oxford days against the wall near the inner door, and his long bookcase. This was packed with books on modern history, politics and economics, and here it was that Bertie would sit typing his long articles on foreign politics. We all knew—and Joyce had told me—how she would go to sleep at night to the sound of "poor Bertie's" typewriter. She was a simple girl, but Bertie was charged by a brain that had given him a Double First at Oxford, made him the master of six or seven languages, and kept him floating for years like an eternal student on scholarships, grants and endowments. In the corner stood stacks of *The Times*, *Le Monde* and other periodicals, on the floor.

"Haven't you caught up on these *yet*?" André said.

"You see, they're sometimes useful," Bertie said. And he added with a stubborn laugh, "Joyce, poor wretch, complains, but I tell her I don't *like* throwing things away."

We moved into the other room.

When I was with Bertie I always felt protective of him, but this evening I did feel a jolt when I saw the dining table, which had been pushed into a far corner of the large room. Those apple pies! Moral questions I found had a way of putting out their noses in small ways in these days. But like everyone else I felt affection for Bertie. He loved his friends and we loved him: he was our possession, and in his shrewd collecting way he felt the same about us. His long nose, on which the glasses never sat straight, his pinkness, his jacket stuffed with papers, pens and pencils, his habit of standing with his hands on his hips as if pretending he had a waist, his short legs apart, his feet restless with self-confidence like a schoolboy keeping goal, were endearing.

His sister-in-law, the only woman to wear a long dress, and her Australian husband were standing in the room.

"And this is William," Bertie said, admiring me. "He's just back from Singapore, idle fellow."

"We have just hopped over from Rome," said Ivy's husband.

Unlike Joyce, Ivy was almost a beauty, the clever businesswoman of the family, and the rest of the evening she seemed to be studying me—so much so that I wondered if Joyce had, in her thoughtless fashion, been talking about us.

We sat around on a deep, frayed sofa or in armchairs in which the cushions had red or green fringes, so that we seemed to be squatting on dyed beards, while Bertie kept us going about people he'd met at the embassy in Brussels, about the rows on the commission—the French delegate walking out in a huff—or a letter in *The Times* in which all the facts were wrong. The dark girl started an

argument about French socialism and Bertie stopped it by saying he
had got in an afternoon's tennis while he was over there.

He was still delighted with us and swaying on his feet, keen on
sending over a volley or smashing a ball over the net. His talk
brought back to me the day he had asked Joyce to marry him. It was
the only proposal of marriage I had ever heard. All of us, except Ivy
and her husband, had been there. We had managed to get one of
the public courts in the Park; on the other courts players were
smartly dressed in their white shorts and we were a shabby lot. I
could see Bertie, who was rolling about like a bundle in old flannels
that were slipping down, and sending over one of his ferocious
services; I could hear him shouting "Well done!" or "Hard luck,
partner!" to Joyce, whose mind strayed if an airplane flew over. I
remembered him sitting beside Joyce and Podge and me on the
bench when our game was over, with one eye on the next game and
the other eye reading a thick political review. It was the time of the
year when the spring green is darkening with the London lead.
Presently I heard him chatting to Joyce about some man, a cousin
of André's who had found an "awfully nice niche" in Luxembourg.
At that time Bertie had found no "niche" and was captivated by
those who had. Joyce had only a vague idea of what a "niche" was
and first of all thought he was talking about churches, but then he
was on to his annual dispute with his solicitor, who wanted him to
get rid of his family's furniture because storage charges were eating
up the trust.

"You see," he said, talking across Joyce and Podge to me, "I shall
want it when I get my London base."

Joyce laughed and said, "But you *are* in London."

"Yes," said Bertie, "but not as a *base*. My argument is that I must
let the stuff stay where it is until I get married."

André and his wife were playing and she had just skied her ball
and, waiting for his moment, André smashed it over. Joyce cried out
"Marvelous!" She had not really been listening to Bertie. And then
she turned to him and said, "I'm sorry. I was watching André—
Bertie, I meant you—you're getting married! How wonderful. I am
so pleased! Who is it? Do tell us."

Bertie gave one of his side glances at Podge and me and then said to Joyce, "You!"

It was really like that: Joyce saying "Don't be silly, Bertie" and "No, I can't. I couldn't . . . I . . ." He got hold of her hand and she pulled it away. "Please, Bertie," she said. She saw, we all saw, he meant it, and she was angry and confused; we saw the other couple coming towards us, their game over. She felt so foolish that she picked up her racket and ran—ran out of the court.

"What's the matter with Joyce?" said André.

Bertie stood up and stared after her and began beating a leg with the review. He appealed to all of us. "I've just asked Joyce to marry me," he said and reported his peculiar approach.

"And she said 'No,' " I said with satisfaction. Love or marriage were far from my own mind; but hearing Bertie and seeing Podge run after Joyce in the Park, I felt a pang of jealousy and loss. In two days I would be far away from my friends, sweating in a job in Singapore. Bertie heard my words, and as always when he was in a jam, he slyly dropped into French. Lightly and confidently he said, *"Souvent femme varie."*

Afterwards it struck me that Bertie's proposal was an appeal: it was the duty of all his friends to get him married. Indeed, Podge said she was afraid he was going to turn to her next. There was even an impression that he had proposed marriage to all of us; but I now see that he was a man with no notion of private life. The team spirit contained his passion, and knowing his exceptional case, he was making us all responsible as witnesses and as friends.

This passed through my mind as we all sat there in his flat listening for the distant ticking of a taxi stopping at the end of the street. Joyce was forbidden to spend money on taxis and would come running in breathlessly saying she had had to "wait hours" for a bus.

Conversation came to a stop. Bertie had at last run down. Suddenly Ivy said, "Bertie, how long was this awful furniture in storage?"

Bertie was not put out. He loved Ivy for calling it awful. He crossed his short, sausagelike legs and sat back with pride in which there was a flash of malice, and flicked his feet up and down.

"Twenty-seven years," he said. "No, let me see. Mother died

when I was born, father died the previous year, then my Aunt Pansy moved in for four or five years, that makes twenty-two years. Yes. Twenty-two."

"I like it," said Podge, defending him.

"But it's unbelievable," said Ivy. "It must have cost a fortune to store it."

"That's what my guardian says," said Bertie.

"Why didn't you make him sell it?" said André.

"I wouldn't let him," said Bertie. "You see, I told him it would be useful when I got married."

We used to say that it must have been the thought of having Bertie's furniture hanging over them that had frightened off the many girls he had tried to marry. After all, a girl wants to choose.

Bertie's pink face fattened with delight at the attack. "Joyce hates it," he said comfortably. "She thinks I ought to sell it."

He was wrong; Joyce laughed at his furniture but she dreaded it.

"You'd make a fortune in Australia with furniture like this," said Ivy's husband.

"No," said Bertie. "You see, it was left to me."

He took off his glasses and exposed his naked face to us. I did not believe Joyce when she told me he cried when she had begged him to sell, but now I did.

If the bedroom had the pathos of an idyll, the furniture in this living room was a hulking manufacture in which historic romance was martial and belligerent. Only in some lost provincial hotel which is putting up a fight against customers do you sometimes find oaken objects of such calumphing fantasy. There was a large armoire with knobs, like breasts, on its pillars and shields on the doors. Under them, sprays of palm leaves had been carved; the top appeared to be fortified. The breast motif appeared on the lower drawers. The piece belonged to the time when cotton manufacturers liked to fancy they lived in castles.

There was a sideboard which attempted the voluptuous, but oak does not flow: shields appeared on its doors. There were more shields carved on two smaller tables; on the dining table, the curved edges would be dangerous to the knuckles, and its legs might have come from the thighs of a Teutonic giantess. The fireplace itself was a battalion of fire irons, toasting forks, and beside it, among other things, two brass scuttles (also with breasts, coats of arms and legs) that stood on claws. There was a general suggestion of jousting mixed with Masonic dinners and ye olde town criers.

"There ought to be a suit of armor," said André.

The only graceful object was Joyce's piano, which had belonged to her mother. It stood there, defeated.

Bertie nodded stubbornly. "You see," he said, grinning at us, "its's my *dot*." And gave a naughty kick with his slippers.

Father dead before he was born, mother dead, aunt dead—Bertie was trebly an orphan. He had been brought up by a childless clergyman who was headmaster of a well-known school. There were photos of school and Oxford groups on the mantelpiece. André and I recognized ourselves in the latter: Bertie was institutional man, his furniture was his only link with common human history. It was the sacred evidence not only of his existence but of the continuity of the bloodstream, the heartbeat and the inextinguishable sexual impulse of his family. He was a rarity, and our rarity too. We were a kind of society for cosseting him. Joyce, who loved him, felt this, and I did too.

But no Joyce came and André cast restless glances at the bottle of sherry, which was now empty. Bertie saw that a distraction was needed. "We can't wait any longer," he said. "Let us eat."

He jumped up, and putting on one of his acts of pantomime, he went to the dining table and picked up a carving knife and fork, and flinging his short arms wide, he pretended to sharpen the knife and then to carve an imaginary roast.

We laughed loudly and Ivy joined him. "Come on!" she said, and pulling *Le Monde* out of his pocket, put it on the dish and said, "Carve this."

Bertie was hurt. "Shame," he said, putting the paper back in his pocket.

Fortunately the front door banged and in came Joyce, breathless, frightened, half laughing, kissing everyone and telling us that Hendrick was giving a lesson when she got there and then would not let her go. And, of course, she had to wait for hours at a bus stop.

"Poor Bertie," she cried and kissed him on the forehead, and shaking her hair, stared back, daring us to say anything that would upset him. She went out to the kitchen and came back to whisper to her sister, "I've got the chops, but I must have left the pud in the taxi. Don't tell him. What shall I do?"

She looked primly at me. She had not changed her clothes, but because she looked prim (and by one of those tricks of the mind) I suddenly saw her standing naked, her long arms freckled, all bones, and standing up to her knees in the water rushing over the rocks of a mountain stream in the North where she and Bertie and I and a climbing party had camped for the night. I was naked too and on the bank, helping her out while Bertie, who refused to go into the river, was standing fully dressed and already, at seven in the morning, with a book he had opened. Bertie was unconcerned.

Yes, I thought this evening as she looked at me—I had one of those revelations that come late to a lover. She stands with the look of a girl who has a strange shame of her bones. She pouts and looks cross as a woman does at an inquisitive, staring child: there is a pause when she does not know what to do, and then she pushes her bones out of her mind and laughs. But that pause has bowled one over. It was because Joyce was so funny to look at that I had become serious about her.

By the time we all sat down to the meal I had advanced to the fantasy that when she laughed, her collarbones laughed. She had quickly changed into a dress that was lower in the neck, so that one saw her long throat. The food was poor; she was no cook, but André had brought wine and soon we were all shouting. Bertie was in full cackle and Joyce was telling us about Hendrick, whom the rest of us had never met, and after dinner Bertie persuaded Joyce to go to the piano and sing one of her French songs.

"Jeune fillette," he called. Quickly, with a flash of nervous intimacy in her glance of obedience, she sat at the piano and began: *"Jeune fillette, profitez du temps . . ."*

Bertie rocked his head as the song came out of her long throat. The voice was small and high, and it seemed to me that she carried it like a crystal inside her. The notes of the accompaniment seemed to come down her arms into her hands—which were really too big —and out of the fingers rather than from the piano. She sang and she played as if she did not exist.

"Her French," André's wife whispered, "is perfect, not like André's awful Belgian accent," and said so again when the song was over.

Joyce had her strange sensual look of having done something wrong.

"She can't speak a word of French," said Bertie enthusiastically. "She was eight months in Paris, staying with Ivy, and couldn't say anything except 'Yes' and 'No.'"

"'No,'" said André, swelling out to tell one of his long Belgian stories, "is the important word."

"You have Mother's voice," Ivy said to Joyce. And to us: "Mother's was small. And true too—and yet she was deaf for the last twenty years of her life. You won't believe it, but Father would sing the solo in church on Sundays and Mother rehearsed him all the week perfectly and yet she can't have heard a note. When she died, Joyce had to do it. And she hated it, didn't you?"

Joy swung around on the stool and now we saw—what I had begun to know too well—a fit of defiance.

"I didn't hate *that*, Ivy," she said. *"You* know what I couldn't bear! On Saturdays," Joyce blurted to us all, daring Ivy to stop her, "after lunch before anything was cleared away, he used to make me get the scissors and clip the hair out of his ears, ready for Sunday."

"Joy!" said Ivy, very annoyed. "You exaggerate."

"I don't," said Joyce. "He used to belch and spit into the fireplace too. He was always spitting. It was disgusting."

We knew that the girls were the daughters of a small builder who had worked his way up and was a mixture of religion and rough habits.

"And so," said Bertie to save the situation, "my future spouse began her *Wanderjahre,* abandoned all and ran away to Paris, where Ivy had established herself—and met the Baron!"

Ivy nodded gratefully. *"Your* baron, Joyce!" she laughed.

"Who is the Baron?" the Australian asked.

Now Joyce appealed to Ivy not to speak, but Bertie told them, mentioning he had met the Baron since those days, in Paris and Amsterdam—Bertie kept in touch with everyone he had ever met. It is painful to hear someone amiably destroy one of the inexpressible episodes in one's life and I knew Joyce was about to suffer, for in one of our confiding afternoons she had tried to tell me. It was true that Ivy, the efficient linguist, had started a translation bureau in Paris and the so-called Baron, a Czech exile, used to dictate long political articles to Joyce. In the long waits while he struggled to translate into English, Joyce's mind was far away.

"He always asked for Joyce," Ivy said. "He used to say—"

"You are not to say it!" said Joyce.

But Ivy mimicked him. "I vant ze girl viz ze beautiful ear. One year in Paris she knows no French, no languages—but she understands. How is zat? She does not listen to ze language. She listens to the Pause!"

"Well done!" cried Bertie.

"What the hell is 'the Pause'?" said the Australian.

"Before he started dictating again," I said brusquely.

Bertie looked at me sharply. I realized I had almost given Joyce away. What I think the Baron was trying to say (I told Joyce when she too had asked me what he meant, for she had grown fond of him and sorry for his family too, whom he had to leave in Prague) was that Joyce had the gift of discontinuity. She was in a dream until the voice that was dictating, or some tune, began again. She and I went on talking about this for a long time without getting any clearer about it, and I agree there was some conceit on my part in this theory: I saw myself as the tune she was waiting for.

"André," Joyce called to hide her anger. "Sing us your song. The awful one."

"It's Bertie's song," said André. "It's his tour de force. Play on, Joyce—and put all the Pauses in."

She could always take a joke from André, who looked like a mottled commissionaire. He had all the beer and Burgundy of Brussels in him, all those mussels, eels and oysters, and that venison.

Bertie's song was one more of his pantomime acts to which his long nose, his eyes darting side glances and his sudden assumption of a nasal voice gave a special lubricity. The song was a rapid cabaret piece about a wedding night in which the bride's shoulder is bitten through, her neck twisted and her arm broken and ends with her mother being called in and saying:

Ci-gît la seule en France
Qui soit morte de cela.

Bertie was devilish as Joyce vamped out the insinuating tune. We all joined in at the tops of our voices in the chorus at the end of each verse:

Ça ne va guère, ça ne va pas

—even Joyce, her little blue eyes sparkling at the words she did not understand, though André had once explained them to her. In the last chorus she glanced back at me, sending me a reckless message. I understood it. From her point of view (and Bertie's), wedding nights were an academic subject. Bertie's enjoyment of the song was odd.

"Really, Bertie!" said the dark girl, who had argued with him about French socialism before dinner.

When she got up from the piano, Joyce looked enviously at her sister because her Australian husband had laughed the loudest and had given Ivy a squeeze. Then as Joyce caught my eye again her strange pout of sensual shame appeared and I felt I had been slapped on the face for having thoughts in my mind that matched her own. Her look told me that I could never know how truly she loved Bertie and feared him too, as she would love and fear a child. And she hated me for knowing what I would never have known unless she had mumbled the tale of tears of failure in the grey room next door.

And a glum stare from Podge, Bertie's oldest friend, showed me even more that I was an outsider.

The song had stirred Bertie's memory too, but of something more remote. He planted himself before me and sprang into yet another of his pantomime acts which the sight of me excited. He put on his baby voice: "William and I didn't have our pudding! Poor Bertie didn't have his pudding."

Joyce's face reddened. Their talk of food, money, their daily domestic life, was irritating in my situation. I lived by my desire; *they* had the intimacy of eating. I must have put on a mask, for Ivy said; "William's all right. He's got his well-fed Chinese look."

Even Joyce had once said that about me.

"How awful of me!" Joyce cried to all of us.

I thought we were lost, but she recovered in time.

"Bertie, isn't it terrible? I left it . . ."—she dared not say "in the taxi"—"I left it at Hendrick's."

Bertie's jollity went. He looked as stubborn as stone at Ivy and Joyce. Then with one of his ingenious cackles he dropped into French, which was a sign of resolution in him. *"Tout s'arrange,"* he said. "You can pick it up on Friday when you go there for rehearsal. By the way, what was it?"

"But, Bertie," Ivy said. "It will be stale or covered in mold by then. Apple tarts."

We all saw a glitter of moisture in Bertie's eyes; it might have come from greed or the streak of miserliness in him—it might have been tears.

"We must get them back," said Bertie.

André saved Joyce by coming out with one of his long detailed stories about a Flemish woman who kept a chicken in her refrigerator for two months after her husband left her. It became greener and greener, and when he came back with his tail between his legs she made him eat it. And he died.

André's stories parodied one's life, but this one distracted Bertie while Joyce whispered to her sister, "He means it."

"Tell him Hendrick ate them. He *has* probably eaten them by now. Singers are always eating."

"That would be worse," said Joyce.

After that André bellowed out a song about his military service and the party broke up. We went into the bedroom and picked up our coats while Joyce stood there rubbing her arms and saying, "Bertie, did you know you had turned out the fire?"

I was trying to signal Friday, Friday, Friday to her, but she took no notice. Of course her sister was staying on in London. How long for? What would that mean?

We all left the house. Bertie stood, legs apart, on the step, triumphant. I found myself having to get a taxi for the socialist girl.

"Where on earth are we?" she asked, looking at the black winter trees and the wet, sooty bushes of the gardens in the street. "Have you known them a long time? Do you live in London?"

"No," I said. "I'm on leave. I work in Singapore."

"What was all that extraordinary talk about the Baron?" She sent up a high laugh. "And the Pause?"

I said it was all Greek to me. I was still thinking Friday, Friday, Friday. Joyce would come or she would not come: more and more reluctant as the day drew nearer, with a weight on her ribs, listening for her tune. And if she heard it, the bones in her legs, arms, her fingers, would wake up and she would be out of breath at my door without knowing it.

TEA
WITH
MRS. BITTELL

She liked to say it was "inconvenient," on the general ground that a lady should appear to complain beautifully when doing a kindness to someone outside her own class; lately she had been keeping an afternoon for a rather "quaint" person, a young man called Sidney, one of a red-jacketed ballet who hopped about at the busy tea counter in Murgatroyd and Foot's. He often chatted with her to annoy the foreign tourists who pushed and shouted at his counter. She discovered that he came on Sundays to her own church. Such a lonely person he was, sitting in his raincoat among the furs and black suits and in such a sad situation: his father had been in the hospital for years now—a coal miner—he had that dreadful thing miners get. It was so *good* that the young man came to church with a friend, another young man from the tea counter, and waking up from her snooze during the service, she often frowned with pleasure. She would say to her atheistical sister, "The younger generation are hungry for Faith." The second young man stopped coming after a month or two, and only Sidney was left. She astounded him by asking him to tea.

Mrs. Bittell was sitting in her flat in the expensive block nearly opposite the church, among the wrongs and relics of her seventy years, when Sidney first came.

"Deliveries round the corner, second door," the doorman said.

"I'm a friend of Mrs. Bittell's," said Sidney.

The doorman's chestload of medals flashed. "Why didn't you say you were a friend?" he said, looking Sidney up and down. "Seventh floor."

"A very disagreeable man," said Mrs. Bittell when Sidney told her this, his wounded chin raised. She was a puddingy woman, reposing on a big sleepy belly; her hair was white and she had innocent blue eyes. She wore, as usual, a loosely knitted pink jersey, low in the neck, a heather-mixture skirt, flat-heeled shoes, and was very short. Her family had been army people and at first she thought Sidney rather civilian in a disappointing way when he was not wearing the red jacket he wore in the shop, as she led him across the wide old-fashioned paneled hall of her flat into the full light of her large drawing room, which, in addition to her furniture and pictures, owned a large part of the London sky where the clouds prospered: one looked down on the tops of three embassies and across to the creamy stucco of a long square.

Sidney sat looking at the distances between her sofas, her satiny chairs and other fine things. She remembered he had been so startled when she invited him to tea that he must be quite outside the concept of "invitations." Indeed, he had gone first of all to one of the large windows and searched the rooftops until he found the building where he and his family distantly lived. It was a high-rise block, a mile away, howling like cats, he told her, with the tenants' radios and television sets and children.

"We don't have anything to do with the neighbors," he said complacently. "Talk to the people next door, next thing they unscrew your front door or saw it off when you go out, and pinch the TV."

He turned his head slowly to Mrs. Bittell. He was a slow-talking young man, nearly handsome in a doleful way, and Mrs. Bittell liked this; she was slow and melancholy herself. He gave a droll laugh when he spoke of doors being sawn off and took a mild pride in the fact.

He also added something about the nearest roofs. "I can't stand slate," he said. "Slate is killing my father. The mine did it."

Mrs. Bittell murmured in her social way that, oh dear, she thought he had been a *coal* miner.

"No," he said. "Slate."

He spoke in short sentences between disconcerting pauses. "Dad took me down when I left school."

"You worked there?" said Mrs. Bittell.

"No," he said fastidiously. "Slate mines are cold. I don't like the cold."

There was a long pause.

"The deeper you go, the colder it gets," he said.

Mrs. Bittell said her sister Dolly had had the same impression of the catacombs outside Rome, even though wearing a coat.

"I've heard of them," he said.

From his account of the mine it seemed to her that he was describing the block of flats in which he was sitting with her, but upside down, under the earth. Yet the mine also seemed like a buried church with aisles, galleries and side chapels, but in darkness and shaken by the noise of drilling holes for the sticks of dynamite and by the explosions in which the echoes pealed from cavern to cavern. The men worked with a stump of lighted candle on the peaks of their caps.

"Surely, Sidney, that is very dangerous, I've been told," said Mrs Bittell. "Not lamps?"

"No gas in the slate mines," he said. But Sidney fell into a state of meditation. "Splinters," he said. "A splinter drops from the roof and goes clean through your skull. You have to wear a helmet. Dad never wore a helmet."

"Oh dear, how thoughtless," said Mrs. Bittell.

"No. A splinter never got him."

Sidney had a taste for horrors which he displayed as part of his family's limited capital. "The dust got him," said Sidney. "He wouldn't wear a mask.

"So I went to work in 'the grocery.'"

Mrs. Bittell was offering him a second cup of tea from her silver teapot. She held the cup above the slop basin.

"I forget, d'you like to keep your remains?"

He thought about this; a funeral appeared to her to be passing through his mind.

"I always keep mine," she said.

"It's okay, Mrs. Bittell," he said.

She was trying to think of a tactful way of saying the accent was on the second syllable of her name.

After that, talk became much easier. His long face still mooned but he warmed, although they got at cross purposes when she thought he was talking about the church when he was talking about the shop. He said he enjoyed the smell of furs, scent—they were like the smell of provisions. He looked at her piano and said, "Do you play it?"

Mrs. Bittell had a wide peaceful white forehead with fine lines on it, her eyes were delicately childlike and her voice was graceful, but now the peacefulness vanished. Her face became square and stub-born, and because his pauses were so long she was tempted to fill them with troubles and horrors of her own: her late husband's atrocious behavior—he had once hit her with a bedside lamp—the selfishness of her daughters, who had made such "hopeless" mar-riages; the suspicions of her trustees, her income not a quarter of what it used to be; the wicked rise of taxes. Her wrongs settled like a migraine in fortified lumps on her forehead. But she did say to Sidney when he mentioned her piano that once one has got used to the big wrongs of life, little ones wake up, with their mean little teeth.

There had been a new wrong in her life in the last few months. The Misses Pattison on the floor below, she told him, the judge on the floor above, a Scottish "banker person," the general across the landing, had complained about her playing the piano. Several ten-ants had sent notes protesting: the landlord and even a solicitor had been dragged in to remind her of Clause 15 in her agreement about the hours when the playing of musical instruments were permitted. She had stonewalled, argued and evaded, tried tears, saying they were depriving an old lady of the only pleasure she had left in life. But she had had to give in: she was allowed to play between two and four in the afternoon. Even the doorman had turned against her. She supposed, she said, Sidney had seen, in the entrance hall to the flats, the board with a sliding slot indicating whether tenants were "In" or "Out." She was sure, she told Sidney, that the doorman changed her slot to "Out" when she was "In," and to "In" when she was "Out."

Sidney came to life when she said this; he exclaimed that the slot said "Out" when he had arrived. Mrs. Bittell had always loved a suspicion and she was impressed to find someone who shared one with her.

Before Sidney came to tea, on all his visits—Wednesday being his day off—Mrs. Bittell sat at her piano, a little distant from it because of her bold stomach, making one more attempt at a bit of Debussy. The notes came slowly from her fingers, for she was not one to vary her pace through life, and with occasional vehemence when she was uncertain. Biting her lips, she tried a little Chopin, but that went too fast, so she moved at last to one of those Hebridean songs she had known since she was a girl of fourteen. Now the fine lines on her forehead cleared and softened, her look became faraway and serene, her eyes became heavenly and she felt herself to be gliding like a lonely bird over the rocky Atlantic shore at Cranach, her grandmother's great house. She was back in her childhood, keeping her father's boat straight in the sea-loch as he stood up and cast his line. She remembered chiefly his moustache like a burn. As the song began to fall away to its end she ventured to sing faintly, her voice coming out strong with longing as she lingered over the last line:

"Sad am I without thee!"

Who was "thee"? Certainly not her father with his shout of "Keep your oars straight, girl"; certainly not her husband, who had helped himself to her money for years and left her contemptuously and gone to live only a mile away across the Park to play bridge with his military friends, and die. Certainly not a lover, though she had once thought the best man at her wedding rather attractive. Not the baby she had lost, or the daughters, who had made such unsuitable marriages. Sometimes she thought of "thee" as a girl—the self that had mysteriously slipped away when she was rushed into her marriage.

The buzzer sounded at the door. "Thee," of course, was not Sidney.

He took off his raincoat, folded it carefully and put it on the chest in the dim hall. They were on closer terms now.

"I heard you playing when I was coming up in the lift," he said.

"Oh dear!" she said.

"Not to worry, Mrs. Bittell. They can't touch you. It's five to four: you've got another five minutes."

And he dawdled to allow her to dash back and get the last ounce of her rights.

He was at ease in the room now.

"Now tell me, how is your father today?" she said.

"The same," he said. "Round at the hospital. He goes three days a week. The doctors think the world of him; he's very popular." He added lazily, "X-rays. He must have had a hundred."

"The family depends on you," she said.

"Oh no," he said. "There was the sickness benefit; the pension; the grant; he's an important case." Sidney seemed to regard the illness as a profession, an investment.

"What a worry for your mother—but you have a sister, haven't you? How old is she? Has she got a job?"

Sidney looked wounded at the suggestion. He was careful to let the peculiarity of his family sink in. "Seventeen," he said. "She sits on the sofa, sucking her thumb, like a baby, and looking at television. She's Mother's pet. They all sit looking at it. Dad too," he said.

This pleased him as he sat thinking about it and he laughed. "Mother goes out," he said, "and always comes back with a special offer she sees on the commercials or something from Bingo.

"That," he added, studying the spaces between things in Mrs. Bittell's flat, in which the well-mannered chairs and tables kept their distance from one another, "is why we're so crowded in our place. You can't cross the room."

Mrs. Bittell said, politely evading comparison, "You have long legs."

"Yes," said Sidney, shaking his head. "Jennifer says, 'You're always on about my legs, what about yours?' "

Sidney offered this information in a bemused way. Suddenly he woke up out of his own life and asked, "Who is that gentleman over there?"

She was relieved to see he was looking at one of three portraits on the wall.

"Oh," she said solemnly, "I thought you meant someone had got into the flat."

"No, hanging on the wall," he said.

"Oh, that's just the old Judge We call him the Judge—the red robe and the fur collar. It was from my mother's family," said Mrs. Bittell in a deprecating way. She had caught Sidney's taste for horrors: "I fear not a very nice man. They say he sentenced his own son to death."

"Oh," Sidney nodded. "History."

"I suppose it is," said Mrs. Bittell. "I like the next one to it, the boy in blue satin with his little sword—the Little Count. I don't know whether he was really a Little Count."

"Is he the one that was sentenced to death?" said Sidney.

"Oh no," said Mrs. Bittell protectively. "The Little Count was the father of the Judge." She had her own pride in her family's crimes.

"Are you interested in pictures?" She got up and he followed her to look more closely.

"Antique," he said. "They must be valuable."

"So they say, but there is such a lot of that sort of thing about," she said.

He gazed a long time at the Little Count and again at the Judge. He gave a sigh. *"The Battle of Waterloo* was on television last night. Did you see it?"

"I'm afraid not," Mrs. Bittell apologized. "I haven't a television. I believe the Misses Pattison have. I can hear it at night." Her wrongs woke up indignantly. "I don't know why they should complain of my piano."

Sidney ignored this. "Do you think the Duke of Wellington was sincere?" he said.

"They say he was very witty," said Mrs. Bittell.

"But do you think he was sincere?"

"Sincere?" said Mrs. Bittell. She was lost. "I've never thought of that," she said.

She saw he was struggling with a moral question, but what was it? She felt one of those violent sensations that swept through her nowadays since her quarrels about the piano. Did Sidney, who was older than she had at first thought, more than thirty, his dark hair receding, did Sidney feel too that sincerity, honesty, consideration, were wearing thin in modern life?

"I know what you mean," said Mrs. Bittell, who did not. She compared Sidney with her ancestors and even with the Duke of Wellington. Sidney was reaching towards the Light; she could not say her forebears had ever done so. She had known the family pictures all her life as furniture: they represented the boredom of centuries, of now meaningless anger. When her husband left her she had seen herself as a woman ruined by generations of reckless plunderers of land, putting down rebellions, fighting wars, gambling and drinking away their money, building big houses, losing their land to

lawyers and farmers, grabbing the money of their wives and quarreling with their children. She saw herself with unassuming pride as the
victim of history. Even in the Mansions—her rising anger told her
—her own class had betrayed her.

She calmed herself by showing him a photograph of a boy of ten.
"My only grandson," she said. "Of course he's grown up now.
Rupert."

"I've got a friend called Rupert," Sidney said.

"Really. Such a nice name," said Mrs. Bittell, putting the photograph down.

"He used to work at Murgatroyd's," he said, suddenly eager. "You
must have seen him—tall, fair moustache. He left."

"I don't remember," she said. "But wait—didn't you bring him
to the church?"

"That's it," said Sidney. "He brought me. You don't often meet
a man who has had an education. Every Sunday we used to go to
a different church—St. Paul's, Westminster Abbey. He knew about
antiques too. Lunchtime and Saturdays we used to go to the National Gallery. He could see *into* pictures. If he was here now," he
said, surveying her pictures and her furniture, "he'd have valued
everything. It was very interesting."

"Very," said Mrs. Bittell.

"I was in the National Gallery this morning," he said. "It's my
day off. I had the idea I might find him there. I've been everywhere
we went. Holborn Baths too, we used to go swimming."

"And did you find him?" said Mrs. Bittell.

"No," said Sidney, looking aloof. "I don't know where he is. He
walked out of the shop last August; not a word."

He paused in the midst of his mystery.

"He left the place where he lived. I went round, but he'd gone.
The landlady didn't know. No address. Not a word."

"Too extraordinary," said Mrs. Bittell.

"I mean, you'd think a friend wouldn't go like that. I thought he
was sincerely my friend." Sidney gazed at her for an answer. "After
three years," he said.

He aged as he gazed. He sat there as if he were the last of a series
of Sidneys who was now quite austerely alone, challenging her with

a slight smile on his mouth, to see the distinction of his case.

"Oh, but there *must* be an explanation, Sidney," said Mrs. Bittell. She had an inspiration. "Was he married? I mean—or was he going to get married?"

Sidney looked at her disparagingly. "Rupert would never marry," he said. "I know that. It was ruin, he always said; you were better alone."

"If it's the wrong person," said Mrs. Bittell, nodding, "but in the Kingdom of Heaven there is neither marriage nor giving in marriage," she said. "As the Bible says." The tune of "Sad Am I Without Thee," went through her head. Her words brought her to the point of confidence, but she did not give in to it.

Sidney considered her. He held his hurt face high. "There was an American who used to come into Murgatroyd's. He was from the Bahamas," he said. "Or somewhere."

"Ah, the Bahamas!" said Mrs. Bittell. "Then perhaps that's where your friend went? My husband's best man went to live in the Bahamas. Have you inquired? Business may have taken him to the Bahamas."

Sidney's pale long face swelled and his mouth collapsed with agonized movements. Mrs. Bittell was embarrassed to see tears on his face.

"I can't bear it, Mrs. Bittell." A loud howl like a dog's howling at the moon came out of him. He was sobbing.

"Oh, Sidney, what is it?" said Mrs. Bittell, moving from her chair to the sofa where he sat.

The cry took her back years to a painful scene in Aldershot when a subaltern in her husband's regiment had suddenly sobbed like this about some wretched girl. He had actually cried on her shoulder. Sidney suddenly did this: his head was on her bosom, weeping. His dark hair had a peculiar smell, just like the subaltern's smell. She patted Sidney on the head, but she was thinking, I mustn't tell my sister Dolly about this, or my daughters. It would be terrible if her grandson suddenly came; he often dropped in.

"I am sure you'll hear from him," she was saying.

"I loved him," Sidney wept.

"Love is never lost. In the Kingdom of Heaven, love is never lost,

Sidney dear," said Mrs. Bittell. "I know how you feel. I have been through it too." She was thinking of her children.

He sat back away from her. He seemed to be saying that whatever she had been through, it was nothing to what he had been through. She also saw that in some kind of craven way he was worshipping her. And even while she felt compassion, she felt disturbed. Why had it never occurred to her, in her miserable troubles with her husband, long ago over and for which her own family blamed her, that there had been no "other woman"?

"We must turn to God," she said, though she knew that years ago she had done nothing of the sort, that outrage had possessed her.

"We must pray," she said. "The Kingdom of Heaven is within us, Sidney." And she declared, "There is no separation for the children of God."

Sidney looked around the room and then back to her, immovable in his gloom.

"We must not cling to our sorrows," she said, for he looked vain of his, but he nodded in a vacant fashion. She smiled beautifully, for she felt that there was some hope in that nod. As he got up to go Sidney changed too. He walked with her into the dim hall, at home in her company now. As he picked up his raincoat he saw himself reflected in the glass of a very large old picture, the full-length portrait of a girl, it seemed, though scarcely visible except for the face.

"Who is that?" he said.

"Oh, just a family thing. It used to be at Cranach. I'll switch on the light."

There was an overshadowing tree with leaves like hundreds of chattering tongues, a little stream in the foreground and a large grey mossy boulder. On it a sad, naked, wooden-looking nymph was sitting, the skin yellowed by time. In one corner of the picture was a little cupid aiming an arrow at her.

Sidney gaped. "Is that you?" he said.

Questions took a long time sinking into Mrs. Bittell's head, which was clouded by kindness and manners and a pride in her relics. She herself had not "seen" the picture for years. It was glazed and was hardly more than a mirror in which she could give a last look at her hat before she went out. She was not surprised by Sidney's remark.

"It doesn't really belong to me, it's really my sister's, but she doesn't like it so I put it there."

Sidney tried to cover his mistake. "That is what I meant. Your sister," he said.

"Oh no," said Mrs. Bittell, waking up. "It's Psyche, the goddess, the nymph, I believe. The Greek legend, Psyche—the soul. I really must get one of those lights they fix to frames. It's so hard to know what to do with big pictures, don't you find? Do you like it?

"It's supposed to be by—Lely, is it?" said Mrs. Bittell nervously. "My husband said it was probably only a copy. My daughter tells me I ought to get it cleaned and hang it in the drawing room, where one can see it more clearly."

The idea appeared to shock Sidney. "I've never seen one like that in a house before. In a gallery. Not in a house," he said censoriously.

"I mean," said Sidney. "The man who painted it, was he sincere?"

Mrs. Bittell was baffled again by the word and murmured politely. Her mind moved as slowly as her feet as she opened the door for him to leave and said, "You must call me Zuilmah, Sidney dear. Remember I will pray for you and Rupert. Ring for the lift," she said.

"I'll go down the stairs," said Sidney. He was bewildered.

She went to the bathroom after he had left and saw from the window the top of the distant block of flats where he lived. Now that the evening was coming on, the block was a tall panel of electric light, standing up in the sky. A thought struck her: How absurd to say it's a portrait of Dolly—no resemblance at all.

She flushed the toilet.

For Mrs. Bittell, Psyche was part of her furniture. She had not really looked at it since she was a girl at Cranach. Then she remembered that she and Dolly used to giggle and say it was Miss Potter, their governess, with nothing on. Mrs. Bittell had long stopped noticing that Psyche was naked, and if she had been asked, would have said that the figure was wearing one of those gauzy scarves that pictures of nymphs wore in books. She had never even thought of naked statues as being naked. Men, she supposed, might think they were—they were so animal.

It came to her that Sidney was a man.

"How embarrassing," she said. She imagined she had seen a hot, reddish cloud in Sidney's eyes. He had gaped, mouth open, at the picture, and his mouth looked angry and wet. She had once or twice seen her wretched husband looking at the picture, mouth open in the same way, though (as she remembered) he was short of money and said, "We'd get a tidy price for it at Christie's," and they had their lifelong quarrel. He was always itching to sell her things to pay his debts.

"You can't sell it, it's Dolly's," she had said to him.

"Your bloody sister," he said.

Now Mrs. Bittell's peaceful face changed into a lump of fear. Sidney slipped into her husband's place and became dangerous. He had had an empty, staring expression when he looked at that body. And he had thought it was she herself! Things she had read in the papers rushed into her mind, tales of men breaking into houses and attacking women, grappling with them, murdering them. Sidney had cried on her shoulder. He had touched her hand. His was hot. The scene became transformed. She saw the struggle. She would scream—she looked at her table with a lamp on it—yes, she would hit him with a lamp. That was what her husband had used on her.

Mrs. Bittell sat on the sofa opposite to the one Sidney and she had sat on and looked at the squashed cushions, her heart thumping. Slowly the panic quietened.

"How foolish," she said.

She recovered and went to her piano. She played three or four notes secretively and sulkily, and the illicit sound restored her.

Of course—Psyche was the soul, a "thee," the thee of her dead baby, herself as a young girl before she married, a loss, sadness. And Sidney too had a "thee." He must have been thinking of Rupert, poor young man.

I must pray. I must not let the Devil get hold of me, she thought. Sidney and Rupert are children of God made in His image and likeness.

And she closed her papery eyelids and prayed and pleasantly dropped off to sleep in the middle of the prayer.

● ● ●

For two weeks Sidney did not come to the church, then he reappeared and came to the flat again.

"I've been worrying about you," she said.

Sidney had changed. She noticed, once he had got out of the dim hall into her drawing room, that his hair was different. It was combed forward and he looked younger, leaner. She did not say anything; perhaps her prayers had been answered.

"I've been worrying about you," she said again. "Have you any news?"

"I made up my mind and packed the job in," he said. He looked careless and grand.

"Sidney! From Murgatroyd's. Was that wise? Why did you do that?" Mrs. Bittell was shocked.

"Undercurrents," he said.

Mrs. Bittell could understand that. There were undercurrents in the Mansions. There were even undercurrents at the church.

"No consideration," he said lazily.

Mrs. Bittell could understand that, too. Why was her youngest daughter so critical of her? Why did young people push past her in bus queues?

"What are you going to do?" she said.

"I'm in no hurry," he said. "I might go back to Reception. Hotels."

"Is that better?" she said.

"Could be," he said.

"That is where I first met him—Rupert—hotel." He was offhand, cool, disdainful.

"Do sit down and tell me," she said.

He sat down. "It's all this stealing that goes on I can't stand. It's not the customers—it's the staff. Food, clocks, rugs—anything. Six Persian rugs last week. You can see it being wheeled off to Delivery and loaded onto vans in the bay. Tell the management, they don't want to know. Insured. Rupert couldn't stand it. I think that's why he left."

"We live in a terrible world," said Mrs. Bittell.

"Bomb in that restaurant yesterday—did you read it in the paper? A woman had her hand blown off," he said.

"How horrible," said Mrs. Bittell. His new haircut made it seem more horrible. "Did they catch the men?"

"Tell the police, they don't want to know," said Sidney.

One of those sudden rages which seized her flared up and made her heart thump; her stomach swelled and her sweet face became ugly. Rage was lifting her into the air. Once more all her wrongs came back to her. She felt herself to be united with him: he was no longer the "quaint" young man. He was human and alone, as she was. And then her rage declined. No, she mustn't give in to anger; one had to face evil. A sentence from one of the vicar's sermons came back to her: she loved the way he said it. "The darkest hour precedes the dawn." This was a dark hour for the world and for Sidney.

"When everything is dark, Sidney dear," she said, "we must pour in more love. We must open the floodgates." She was swimming in the growing exaltation of one who had sent out a message. She looked at his doubting face.

A vulgar buzzer went at the door which startled her.

"Oh dear," said Mrs. Bittell. "Now, who can that be? I hope it is not someone awkward."

How often in her life she had expected a prayer to be miraculously answered when she opened her eyes.

Sidney and she looked at each other. Then her face became stubborn. "How irritating," she said. "I'm losing my memory. It's Mr. Ferney. I'd forgotten him. He's a friend of my sister's and we've drunk all the tea. How silly of me."

"Shall I go to the door?" said Sidney possessively.

"No, I'll go. He's retired," she called back as she went. "Stay here. Would you do me a great kindness and put the kettle on? Wait—it's probably the doorman."

Mr. Ferney was at the door. Mr. Ferney was a meaty middle-aged man with two reproachful chins and a loud flourishing voice.

"Dear Zuilmah," he bawled. "Always the same. Like your Psyche, with a lily in your hand, waiting for Cupid's arrow. Am I late?"

"We didn't wait for you," said Mrs. Bittell.

Since he had retired Mr. Ferney's profession was having tea with ladies. He was on the verge of a belated search for a wife.

"You don't know Mr. Taplow, a dear friend," said Mrs. Bittell. Mrs. Bittell went to make more tea.

"Tiplow," said Mr. Ferney. "Somerset Tiplows?"

"Taplow," said Sidney.

"Taplow, Tiplow, all Somerset names. Tiplawn, too. People couldn't spell in the past. You'll find Ferns, Fennys, de la Fresne and of course Ferness. I tell Mrs. Bittell that she was a Battle," he confided in a loud voice. "Bataille."

"What are you talking about?" said Mrs. Bittell, returning with her silver teapot.

"Your horrible family, my dear," said Mr. Ferney. "The rogues' gallery—that awful fellow." He pointed to the Judge.

"Mr. Taplow and I were talking about that the other day, weren't we, Sidney? Sidney was saying that History is coming back, wasn't that it? Tell Mr. Ferney."

"History always comes back. I can't afford it, can you?" said Mr. Ferney.

Sidney's face became swollen on one side and he said, "I'll be going, then. I've got to get Father," to Mrs. Bittell.

"Must you? Oh dear. Of course you must," said Mrs. Bittell. "Mr. Taplow's father is in the hospital."

"Nothing serious, I hope."

"I'm afraid it is," said Mrs. Bittell.

"Such a tiresome man, I'm so sorry," she murmured as she took Sidney to the door. "Remember, Sidney dear, what I said. Open the floodgates. Don't forget to come to church on Sunday."

And seeing his unhappy look, she gave him a light kiss.

Sidney was shocked by the kiss.

"Who is that? What's he mean by 'then'? I've seen him somewhere. It'll come back to me . . . Treplawn," said Mr. Ferney.

"He used to work at Murgatroyd and Foot's," said Mrs. Bittell. "Terrible stories he's been telling me. I'm trying to help him."

"Oh, I see," said Mr. Ferney, relieved, and passed his cup. "What's he after? You do slave for people. I wish you'd slave for me."

• • •

Thieves in Murgatroyd and Foot's, a shop known all over the world for generations! The building itself became a long flaunting wrong and, for her, London changed overnight. Even the gardens in the squares became suspect to her. The doors of pillared terraces looked dubious, embassies were white sepulchres, the cars outside hotels carried loads of criminals away. Walking in her quiet way, in the past she had floated sedately above curiosity, merely noticing that the young rushed. But now she saw that the city had become a swarming bazaar: swarms of foreigners of all colors—Arabs, Indians, Chinese, Japanese, and all people jabbering languages she had never heard—came in phalanxes down the pavements, their eyes avid for loot. If she paused because she heard an English voice, she was pushed and trodden on, more than once laughed at. In the once quiet streets, such as the one in which her sister lived, there were empty bottles of whisky and brandy rolling in the gardens.

She noticed these things now because for three weeks Sidney had not been to church and when she was out walking she was looking at all the faces thinking she might see him. He had disappeared in the flood.

Yet, the more impossible it was for her to know where he was or what he was doing or why he did not come, the calmer she became; inevitably the divine will would be manifested and, indeed, she went so far as to stop praying; in a modest way the sensation was exalting.

At church she gave up looking for Sidney in the congregation when the hymns were sung—she was too short to see far when she was sitting. It must have been on the fifth Sunday, as she stood up for the second hymn and heard the mouths of the well-dressed congregation shouting forth, that she noticed two men across the aisle who were holding their hymnbooks high and not singing. Sidney—and who was the other man? She hardly remembered him— it *must* be Rupert!

Mrs. Bittell stopped singing and said loudly, almost shouted "No" to the will of God. She flopped into her seat and her umbrella went to the floor. The church seemed to roll like a ship; the altar shot up into the air. The powerful odor of the fur coat of the woman in front of her was suffocating. The miracle had occurred. Rupert had returned. Sidney was standing beside him. Prayer had been answered:

it had swept Rupert back across the Atlantic. All the old prayers of her life that had never been answered became like rubbish. A real miracle had been granted to her.

Flustered, she got to her feet and started singing the last verse and looked across the aisle. The two young men had heard her umbrella fall and now they were both singing, and singing at her, at least Rupert's mouth was open but Sidney was half hidden, and Rupert's teeth flashed. She nodded curtly; she had only one desire: to go at once across the aisle in anger and say, "Why didn't you tell Sidney you were going away? Why didn't you write? If he is sincerely your friend?"

When the service was over, they were ahead of her in the crowded aisle, but she found Sidney waiting for her on the pavement and Rupert a few yards away.

"He's back," said Sidney, beckoning to Rupert, who stood politely aside. For a moment the young man still looked unlike a real man but more like some photograph of a man.

"What did I tell you, Sidney?" she said as Rupert came nearer.

Sidney stood back, gazing up at the hero, his eyes begging her to admire.

"I remember you, Mrs. Bittell," Rupert said.

"What a time it has been," she said.

"What a time," he said.

"Our bus," said Sidney.

"You must tell me everything. Come to tea," she pleaded. "Monday? I don't want to lose you again."

They looked at each other and glanced at the bus and agreed. How flat she felt, but as they ran for the bus they turned back to wave—how delightful to see a miracle running.

Mrs. Bittell went beautifully and as if empowered to the door. There stood Sidney, so proud that he looked as if he would fall headfirst into the hall; behind him, stiffly controlled, stood Rupert, the answered prayer, perhaps rightly wearing dark glasses as if, as yet, shy of the spiritual life. She forgot to close the door and Rupert politely shut it for her.

"It gives a click," she called back to him.

"It clicked," he said.

Sidney went eagerly forward. They stood in the drawing room.

"The Judge!" said Sidney, pointing to the picture. Rupert ignored this and looked around the room.

"Now," said Mrs. Bittell playfully, "where is your sunburn?"

"He has been ill," said Sidney. "He's only just out of the hospital."

"I picked up one of those bugs," said Rupert.

"Oh dear. I hope it was not serious," said Mrs. Bittell.

"Two months," said Sidney dramatically. What an emotional young man he was!

It was disappointing not to see the miracle in perfect health. His voice was hoarse, he brought a smell of cigarettes with him and he had lost weight, so that his cocoa-colored suit was loose on him. His thin face seemed to have a frost on it, and when he took his dark glasses off, he was obliged to narrow his eyes because of the light in the room. The thinness of the face made his mouth and lips too wide. There was grey in his hair. She noticed this because she had never been sure which of the young men at the tea counter he was. He sat so stiff and still, and despite his illness, his bones looked too heavy for the chair. He picked up one of the cups on the tea table and looked at the mark as Mrs. Bittell went off to get her silver teapot.

"Now tell us all about the Bahamas," said Mrs. Bittell as she came back, and out came her story that her husband's best man at their wedding had been ADC to the Governor, whose name she could not remember; it was a long time ago, of course.

"Who is Governor now?"

The question made Rupert smile thoughtfully. "McWhirter," he said at last. "He's retired, though—not very popular—the new man came after I left."

"I must ask my sister. She'll tell us," said Mrs. Bittell.

This was disappointing. And Rupert's account of the Bahamas was bewildering. No Government House, no beaches, no palm trees. All Victorians, he said. Full of English stuff left by early settlers. Harmoniums everywhere, he said, grandfather's clocks. Fox-hunting pictures.

Sidney said enthusiastically that Rupert was "in antiques."

Mrs. Bittell recovered. "There used to be Bittells in sugar—though I believe that was in Jamaica." She spoke disdainfully, admitting—to put Rupert at his ease—the shames that can occur in all families. She moved nearer home. "You must be very thankful you left Murgatroyd's," she said, admiring him. "There were undercurrents, Sidney tells me."

Rupert said, "You could put it that way."

"It takes courage," she said and she meant this for Sidney, for it seemed to her that Rupert was a decisive man, one who had struck out on his own.

"You have interesting things," he said, nodding at her very fine bureau.

"Just old things from Cranach," said Mrs. Bittell and she led them across the room.

"These are large flats," he said. "You've got a museum."

"And there's the big picture in the hall," said Sidney, the excited familiar of the place. "Lily."

They went out into the hall and Rupert looked closely at the picture. "It could be a Lely," he said.

An educated man!

And then Rupert said something which was not really very tactful. "It would pay you to have this cleaned," he said. "Six by four," he said, guessing the measurements. "It needn't cost too much if you go to the right firm—Dolland's, say—they do a good job. I mean, it would bring it out."

"I do not think my sister would care for that," Mrs. Bittell said. "It has never been cleaned. You see, it's always been in the family. I believe it was always like that."

She did not think Rupert knew her well enough to make suggestions about the tastes of the Bittells. They did not like things "brought out." She certainly did not wish to do anything as "inconvenient" as that. It would be like asking Dolly to get herself "brought out."

"It's very suitable with the paneling," she said.

"That's true enough," said Rupert disparagingly.

And then Rupert made one more worrying remark about the

picture. It was, she reported to her sister more than once afterwards, kindly meant, she was sure.

"That's interesting. There's one in the National Gallery like this, Sid." (He called Sidney "Sid"!) "See the cupid down there in the corner? See how he's holding his bow? He's going to miss. He won't get her in the heart. He'll catch her in the—er—leg," he said. And he indicated the probable course of the arrow. And he gave a short laugh.

Over the years Mrs. Bittell had not particularly noticed that Psyche had a leg. Surely it was quite wrong to believe that the soul had legs.

And she could not understand why Rupert laughed.

She said, in her social voice, as one asking for information, "I always understood Cupid was blind."

Rupert stopped his laugh and she was amazed to see him turn to Sidney and do a most disconcerting thing: he winked at Sidney. The answer to prayer had winked. Even Sidney, she saw, was shocked by this.

Soon after this they said goodbye.

The miracle had vanished. The flat was empty now. Rupert had come back. Sidney was happy. There was nothing for her to do. He did not come to church. His visits stopped.

"Sad am I without thee"—whoever "thee" was—she sang on some days as she played her piano in the agreed hours. That last chord became more vehement. Mrs. Bittell put jealousy into the chord. Surely Sidney could spare her one afternoon? The hardest aspect of the case was that she had no one left to pray for, but she was stubborn in her sense of loss and she began to feel, as her jealousy grew, that wherever Sidney was, whatever he was doing, she could still pray for the freedom of his soul. Freedom, of course, from that very puzzling love of that strange young man who had, after all, not been sincere.

It was a prayer without urgency. It would come into her head at night when she saw the lights of the flats where Sidney lived, or when she was visiting her sister, or sitting on the train coming home from one of those trying visits to her daughter.

On one of her returns, on a Sunday too, when she had been obliged to miss her church, at six in the afternoon—she was expecting her grandson. She feared she was late. She got to her flat. She *was* late. The boy was there. His suitcase was in the hall, open, in his untidy way and—strange—his shoes beside it.

"Rupert darling," she called.

And when there was no answer, she called again. There was a strange smell in the flat. But then there were sounds; he must be in the bathroom. She went to the bathroom door and said quietly, "Rupert. It's Granny."

The door was open. He was not there. She went to her bedroom, where the door was half open, and there she saw a pair of stockinged feet and the cocoa-colored trousers of a man kneeling at a drawer beside her bed.

"What *are* you doing, Rupert?" she said. The man got halfway to his feet.

She saw the face of Sidney's Rupert. His dark glasses were on her bed with some of her jewelry. A long smile split his face for a moment as he stood up. He had a bracelet in his hand.

"Put that down," said Mrs. Bittell. And called calmly, as if to her grandson, "Rupert, there's a man in my bedroom."

And with that she pulled the bedroom door to and turned the key in the lock.

"I've locked him in," she called.

The man was wrenching at the door handle. Then she heard him open the window.

But now Mrs. Bittell had exhausted the words she could speak. She opened her mouth to scream, but no sound came. Lead seemed to fill her legs, her heart thundered in her ears; she saw through the doorway of the drawing room (miles away it seemed) the telephone. She began a slow trudge that seemed to take hours, as in a dream, while the man returned to hammering at the door, shouting, "I'll break your bloody neck, you silly old bitch."

She was stupefied enough to turn and hear the sentence out. She got to the drawing room, then to the hall, and what she saw there drove her back. Psyche was not there. The frame was empty. That sight drove her back, and giddily she went to her piano and banged away at the keys, defying the whole block of flats, banging as the man banged at the closed door. The telephone rang and rang, but still she banged and banged on the keys and then the man broke through the door and was coming at her, but in his stockinged feet; on the parquet at the edge of one of her rugs he skidded and fell flat on his back.

Mrs. Bittell saw this. She had often, in her quiet way, thought of what she would do if someone attacked her. She had always planned to speak gently and to ask them why they were so unhappy and had they forgotten they were children of God. But a terrible thing had happened. She had wet herself, like a child, all down her legs. Red with shame, as he rushed and fell and was trying to get up, she tipped the piano stool over as he jumped at her. He stumbled over it. And this was the moment she had often imagined. She became as strong as History; she picked up the brass table lamp and bashed him on the neck, the head, anywhere. Not once, but twice or three times. And then fell back and fainted.

That is how the doorman, the general from across the landing, the Misses Pattison and her grandson found her, as Rupert, bleeding in the head, was trying to put on his shoes in the hall and run for it.

"Tell Sidney to come," she was murmuring as they knelt beside her, and for a long time the telephone still went on ringing.

"A man called Sidney," said the doorman, answering it. "He's asking for her."

He turned to the crowd. "He says it's urgent."

No one replied.

With pomp the doorman returned to the telephone and said, "Mrs. Bittell is indisposed."

THE
FIG TREE

I checked the greenhouses, saw the hose taps were turned off, fed the Alsatian and then put the bar on the main gate to the Nursery and left by the side door for my flat. As I changed out of my working clothes I looked down on the rows of labeled fresh green plants. What a pleasure to see such an orderly population of growing things gambling for life—how surprising that twenty years ago the sight of so much husbandry would have bored me.

When I was drying myself in the bathroom I noticed Sally's bathcap hanging there and I took the thing to the closet in the bedroom, and then in half an hour I picked up Mother at her hotel and drove her to Duggie and Sally's house, where we were to have dinner. I supposed Mother must have seen Sally's bathcap, for as we passed the Zoo she said, "I do wish you would get married again and settle down."

"Dutch elm disease," I replied, pointing to the crosses on one or two trees in the Park.

The Zoo is my halfway mark when I go to Duggie and Sally's—what vestiges of embarrassment I feel become irrelevant when I pass it.

"It worries your father," Mother said.

Mother is not "failing." She is in her late seventies and Father was killed in the war thirty years ago, but he comes to life in a random way, as if time were circular for her. Father seems to be wafted by, and sows the only important guilt I have—I have so little memory of him. Duggie has said once or twice to Sally that though I am in my early forties, there are still signs that I lacked a father's discipline. Duggie, a speculative man, puts the early whiteness of my hair down to this. Obviously, he says, I was a late child, probably low in vitality.

Several times during this week's visit I have taken Mother around the shops she likes in London. She moves fast on her thin legs, and if age has shortened her by giving her a small hump on her shoulders, this adds to her sharp-eyed, foraging appearance. She was rude, as usual, to the shop assistants, who seemed to admire this—perhaps because it reminded them of what they had heard of "the good old days." And she dressed with taste, her make-up was delicate, and if her skin had aged, it was fine as silk; her nose was young, her eyes as neat as violets. The week had been hot, but she was cool and slightly scented.

"Not as hot as we had it in Cairo when your father was alive," she said in her mannish voice.

Time was restored: Father had returned to his grave.

After being gashed by bombs during the war, the corner of early-Victorian London where Duggie and Sally live has "gone up." Once a neighborhood of bed-sitters, now the small houses are expensive and trim; enormous plane trees, fast-growing sycamores, old apple and pear trees bearing uneatable fruit, crowd the large gardens. It was to see the garden and to meet Duggie, who was over from Brussels on one of his monthly trips, that Mother had really come: in the country she is an indefatigable gardener. So is Sally, who opened the door to us. One of the unspoken rules of Sally and myself is that we do not kiss when I go to her house; her eyes were as polite as glass (and without that quiver to the pupils they usually have in them) as she gave her hand to my mother. She had drawn her fair hair severely back.

"Duggie is down in the garden," Sally said to Mother and made a fuss about the steps that lead down from her sitting-room balcony. "These steps my husband put in are shaky—let me help you."

"I got used to companionways going to Egypt," said Mother in her experienced voice. "We always went by sea, of course. What a lovely garden."

"Very wild," said Sally. "There used to be a lawn here. It was no good, so we dug it up."

"No one can afford lawns nowadays," said my mother. "We have three. Much better to let nature take its course."

It is a clever garden, of the romantic kind, half of it a green cavern under the large trees where the sun can still flicker in the higher branches. You duck your way under untidy climbing roses; there is a foreground, according to season, of overgrown marguerites, tobacco plants, dahlias, irises, lilies, ferns—a garden of wild, contrived masses. Our progress was slow as Mother paused to botanize until we got to a wide, flagged circle which is shaded by a muscular fig tree. Duggie was standing by the chairs with a drink in his hand, waiting for us. He moved a chair for Mother.

"No, I must see it all first," Mother said. "Nice little magnolia." I was glad she noticed that.

There was a further tour of plants that "do well in the shade"— "Dear Solomon's-seal," she said politely, as if the plant were a person. A bird or two darted off into other gardens with the news —and then we returned to the chairs set out on the paved circle. Duggie handed drinks to us, with the small bow of a tall man. He is lazily well-made, a bufferish fellow in his late fifties, his drooping grey moustache is affable—"honorable" is how I would describe the broad road of sunburned baldness going over his head. His nose is just a touch bottled, which gives him the gentlemanly air of an old club servant, or rather of being not one man but a whole club, uttering impressions of this and that. Out of this club his private face will appear, a face that puts on a sudden, fishy-eyed stare, in the middle of one of his long sentences. It is the stare of a man in a brief state of shock who has found himself suspended over a hole that has opened at his feet. His job takes him abroad a good deal and his stare is also that of an Englishman abroad who has sighted another Englishman he cannot quite place. Not being able to get a word in while the two women were talking, he turned this stare on me. "I missed you the last time I was home," he said.

Again, it is my rule that I don't go to the house unless he is there.

"How is that chest of yours?"

I gave a small cough and he gave me a dominating look. He likes to worry about my health.

"The best thing your uncle ever did for you was to get you out of the City. You needed an open-air life."

Duggie, who has had to make his own way, rather admires me for having had a rich uncle.

Was he shooting a barb into me? I don't think so. We always have this conversation: he was born to repeat himself—one more sign of his honorableness.

Duggie takes pride in a possessive knowledge of my career. He often says to Sally, "He ought to put on weight—white hair at his age—but what do you expect? Jazz bands in Paris and London, hanging round Chelsea bars, playing at all that literary stuff, going into that bank—all that sort of nonsense." Then he goes on, "Mother's boy—marrying a woman twelve years older than himself. Sad that she died," he adds. "Must have done something to him— that breakdown, a year in the sanatorium, he probably gambled. Still, the Nursery has pulled him together. Characteristic, of course, that most of the staff are girls."

"It's doing well," he said in a loud confidential voice, nodding at the fig tree by the south wall, close to us.

"What a lovely tree," Mother said. "Does it bear? My husband will only eat figs fresh from the tree."

"One or two little ones. But they turn yellow and drop off in June," said Sally.

"What it needs," Duggie said, "is the Mediterranean sun. It ought to be in Turkey, that is where you get the best figs."

"The sun isn't enough. The fig needs good drainage and has to be fertilized," mother said.

"All fruit needs that," said Duggie.

"The fig needs two flies—the Blastophaga and, let me see, is it the Sycophaga? I think so—anyway, they are Hymenoptera," Mother said.

Duggie gazed with admiration at my mother. He loves experts. He had been begging me for years to bring her over to his house.

"Well, we saved its life, didn't we, Teddy?" he said to me and boasted on his behalf and mine. "We flagged the area. There was nothing but a lake of muddy water here. How many years ago was that?"

"Four or five," I said.

"No!" said Duggie. "Only three."

Was he coming into the open at last and telling me that he knew that this was the time when Sally and I became lovers? I think not. The stare dropped out of his face. His honorable look returned.

Sally and Duggie were what I call "Monday people" at the Nursery. There is a rush of customers on the weekend. They are the instant gardeners who drive in, especially in the spring and autumn, to buy everything, from plants already in bud and flowers, the potted plants, for balconies of flats. The crowd swarms and our girls are busy at the counter we had to install to save costs as the business grew. (The counter was Duggie's idea: he could not resist seeing the Nursery as one of his colonies.) But on Monday the few fanatic gardeners come, and I first became aware of Sally because she was very early, usually alone, a slight woman in her late thirties with her straw-blond hair drawn back from a high forehead in those days, a severe look of polite, silent impatience which would turn into a wide, fastidious grimace like the yawn of a cat if anyone spoke to her. She would take a short step back and consider one's voice. She looked almost reckless and younger when she put on glasses to read what was on the sacks and packets of soil, compost and fertilizer in the store next to the office, happiest in our warm greenhouses, a woman best seen under glass. Her eyebrows were softer, more downily inti-mate than anything else about her. They reminded me when I first saw her of the disturbing eyebrows of an aunt of mine which used to make me blush when I was a boy. Hair disturbs me.

One day she brought Duggie to the Nursery when I was unloading boxes of plants that came from the growers and I heard her snap at him, "Wait here. If you see the manager, ask about grass seed and stop following me around. You fuss me."

For the next half-hour she looked around the seedlings or went into the greenhouses while Duggie stood where he was told to stand. I was near him when the lorry drove off.

"Are you being attended to?" I said. "I'll call a girl."

He was in his suspended state. "No, I was thinking," he said in the lazy voice of a man who, home from abroad and with nothing to do, was hoping to find out if there were any fellow thinkers about. "I was thinking, vegetation is a curious thing," he said with the predatory look of a man who had an interesting empire of subjects to offer. "I mean, one notices when one gets back to London there is more vegetation than brick. Trees," he said. "Plants and shrubs, creeper, moss, ivy," he went on, "grass, of course. Why this and not that? Climate, I suppose. You have laurels here, but no oleander, yet it's all over the Mediterranean and Mexico. You get your fig or your castor-oil plant, but no banana, no ginkgo, no datura. The vine used to swarm in Elizabethan times, but rare now, but I hear they're making wine again. It must be thin. The climate changed when the Romans cut down the forests." For a moment he became a Roman and then drifted on, "Or the Normans. We all come down to grass in the end."

He looked at our greenhouses.

"My job takes me away a lot. I spend half the year abroad," he said. "Oil. Kuwait."

He nodded to the distant figure of his wife. She was bending over a bed of tobacco plants.

"We spent our honeymoon in Yucatán," he said with some modest pomp. He was one of those colonizing talkers, talking over new territory.

"But that is not the point," he said. "We can't get the right grass seed. She sows every year, but half of it dies by the time summer comes. Yet, look at the Argentina pampas." He was imposing another geography, some personal flora of his own, on my Nursery. Clearly not a gardener: a thinker at large.

I gave him the usual advice. I took him to a shed to show him sacks of chemicals. His wife came back from the flower beds and found us. "I've been looking for you everywhere," she said to him. "I told you to wait where you were." She sounded to be an irritable woman.

He said to me, in an aloof, conspiring way, ignoring her, "I suppose you wouldn't have time to drop round and have a look at our lawn? I mean, in the next week or two—"

"It will be too late by then," she interrupted. "The grass will be dead. Come along," and she made that grimace—a grimace that now struck me as a confidence, an offhand intimation.

He made an apologetic gesture to me and followed her obediently out of the Nursery.

I often had a word or two with Sally when she came alone: grass seed seemed to be the couple's obsession. She said it was his; he said it was hers. I was a kind of umpire to whom they appealed when we met.

So one afternoon in November when I was delivering laurels to a neighbor of theirs down the street, I dropped in at their house.

A fat young man was sitting sedately on a motorbike outside it, slowly taking off a fine pair of gauntlets. Sitting behind the screen of the machine, he might have been admiring himself at a dressing-table mirror. In his white crash helmet he looked like a doll, but one with a small black moustache.

"Those lads get themselves up, don't they?" I said to Duggie, who came to the door.

"Our tenant," Duggie said. "He has the flat in the basement. He uses the side entrance. Under our agreement he does not use the garden. That is reserved for ourselves. Come through—I had these iron steps put in so that my wife has strictly private access to the garden without our interfering with him or he with us. My wife would have preferred a young married couple, but as I pointed out, there would be children. One has to weigh one thing against another in this life—don't you find?"

We went down to the garden. Their trouble was plain. The trees were bare. Half of the place was lifeless soil, London-black and empty. The damp yellow leaves of the fig tree hung down like wretched rags, and the rest had fallen flat as plates into a very large pool of muddy water that stretched from one side of the garden to the other. Overnight, in November, a fig collapses like some Victorian heroine. Here—as if she were about to drown herself. I said this to Duggie, who said, "Heroine? I don't follow."

"You'll never grow a lawn here. Too much shade. You could cut the trees down . . ."

At this moment Sally came down and said, "I won't have my trees cut down. It's the water that's killing everything."

I said that whole districts of London were floating on water. Springs everywhere, and the clay held it.

"And also, the old Fleet River runs underground in this district," I said. "The only thing you can do is to put paving down."

"The Fleet River? News to me," said Duggie and he looked about us at other gardens and houses as if eager to call out all his neighbors and tell them. "Pave it, you say? You mean with stones?"

"What else?" said Sally curtly and walked away. The garden was hers.

"But, my dear," he called after her, "the point is—what stones? Portland? Limestone?"

The colonizer of vegetation was also a collector of rock. A load of geology poured out of him. He ran through sandstone, millstone, grit, until we moved on to the whinstone the Romans used on Hadrian's Wall, went on to the marble quarries of Italy and came back to the low brick wall of their garden, which had been damaged during the war.

Presently there was the howling and thumping of jazz music from the basement flat.

"I told you that man has girls down there," Sally said angrily to her husband. "He's just come in. He's turning the place into a discotheque. Tell him to stop—it's intolerable."

And she looked coldly at me as if I too were a trespasser, the sort of man who would kick up a shindy with girls in a quiet house. I left. Not a happy pair.

I sent him an estimate for paving part of the garden. Several months passed; there was no reply and his wife stopped coming to the Nursery. I thought they were abroad. Then in the spring Duggie came to the Nursery with his daughter, a schoolgirl, who went off to make up confidently to a van driver.

Duggie watched her and then said to me, "About those paving stones. My wife has been ill. I had a cable and flew home."

"I hope it was not serious?"

He studied me, considering whether to tell me the details, but evidently—and with that kind of reluctance which suggests all—changed his mind. "The iniquitous Rent Act," he said disparagingly, "was at the bottom of it."

He gave an outline of the act, with comments on rents in general.

"Our tenant—that boy was impossible, every kind of impertinence. We tried to get rid of him but we couldn't. The fellow took us to court."

"Did you get an order against him?" I asked.

Duggie's voice hurried. "No. Poor fellow was killed. Drove his motorbike head-on into a lorry, a girl with him too. Both killed. Horrible. Naturally, it upset my wife: she blames herself. Imagination," he apologized. Duggie spoke of the imagination accusingly.

"The man with the little black moustache?" I asked.

"She wouldn't have a married couple there," he said.

"I remember," I said. "You mentioned it."

"Did I?" he said. He was cheered by my remembering that.

"You see," he said. "It was clearly laid down in the agreement that he was not to go into the garden under any pretext, but he did. However, that is not what I came about. We're going to pave that place, as you suggested. It will take her mind off it all." He nodded to the house. "By the way, you won't say anything to her, will you? I'm away so much the garden is everything to her."

Shortly after this I took one of our men over to the house. Duggie was stirred at the end of the first day when he came home from his London office to see we had dug up a lot of brick rubble—chunks of the garden wall which had been knocked down by blast during the war. On the second day he came back early in the afternoon and stood watching. He was longing to get hold of my man's pickaxe. The man put it down and I had turned around when I heard the dead sound of steel on stone and a shout of "Christ!" from Duggie. He had taken the pickaxe and brought it down hard on a large slab of concrete and was doubled up, gripping his wrists between his legs, in agony. Sally came to the balcony and then hurried down the steps. Her appearance had changed. She was plumper than she had been, there was no sign of illness and she had done her hair in a new way: it was loosened and she often pushed it back from her cheeks.

"You are a fool, Duggie," she said.

The man was shoveling earth clear of the slab of concrete, which tilted down deep into the earth.

"It's all right. It's all right. Go away. I'm all right," said Duggie.

"What is it?" he said.

"Bleeding air-raid shelter," my gardener said. "There's one or two left in the gardens round here. A gentleman down the road turned his into a lily pond."

He went on shoveling and dug a hole. The concrete ended in a tangle of wire and stone. It had been smashed. He kneeled down on the ground and said, "The end wall has caved in, full of wet muck," he said. He got up and said, disappointed, "No one in it. Saved some poor bloke's life. If he copped it, he wouldn't have known, anyway."

Sally made a face of horror at the gardener. "Those poor people," she said. "Come indoors. What a fool you are, Duggie."

Duggie refused to go. Pain had put him in a trance: one could almost see bits of his mind traveling out of him as he called triumphantly to her, "Don't you see what we've got, my dearest?" he cried, excitement driving out his pain. He was a man whose mind was stored with a number of exotic words: "We've got a *cenote.*"

How often we were to hear that word in the next few days! For months after this he must have continued startling people with it in his office, on buses, men in clubs, whoever was sitting next to him in aircraft on his way to Kuwait.

"What is a cenote?" I said, no doubt as they did.

"It's an underground cistern," he said. "You remember Yucatán, Sally—all those forests, yet no water. No big rivers. You said, 'How did the Mayas survive?' The answer was that the Maya civilization floated on underground cisterns."

Duggie turned to me, calling me Teddy for the first time. "I remember what you said about London floating on underground rivers—it's been on my mind ever since you said it. Something was there at the back of my mind, some memory, I couldn't get it. There it is: a cenote. That's where your fig tree has been drinking, Sally. You plant your fig tree on a tank of water and the rubble drains it.

"Sally and I saw dozens of cenotes, all sizes, some hundred feet deep on our honeymoon," he confided to me.

Sally's eyes went hard.

"The Mayans worshipped them: you can see why. Once a year the priests used to cut out the heart of a virgin and throw it into the water. Propitiation," he said.

"It's an act for tourists at the night clubs there," said Sally drearily.

"Yes," Duggie explained to us and added to me, "Fake, of course."

Sally said, "Those poor people. I shall never go into this garden again."

In the next few days she did not come down while we turned the ruin into a foundation, and the following week Duggie superintended the laying of the stones. His right arm was in a sling.

When the job was finished Duggie was proud of the wide circle of stones we had laid down.

"You've turned my garden into a cemetery. I've seen it from the window," Sally said.

Duggie and I looked at each other: two men agreeing to share the unfair blame. She had been ill; we had done this job for her and it had made things worse.

Imagination, as Duggie had said. Difficult for him. And I had thought of her as a calm, sensible woman.

It happened at this time I had to go to the Town Hall about a contract for replanting one of the neglected squares in the borough, and while I was there and thinking of Duggie and Sally I tried to find out who had lived in their house and whether there was any record of air-raid casualties. I went from office to office and discovered nothing. Probably the wrong place to go to. Old cities are piled on layer after layer of unrecorded human lives and things. Then Duggie sent a check for our work, more promptly too than most of our customers do. I thought of my buried wife and the rot of the grave as I made out a receipt. It occurred to me that it would be decent to do something for Duggie. I was walking around the Nursery one morning when I saw a small strong magnolia, a plant three feet high and already in bud. It was risky to replant it at this time, but I bound it, packed it and put it in a large tub and drove to their house one Saturday with it, to surprise them. Sally came to the door with a pen in her hand and looked put-out by my sudden call. I told her I had the plant in the van.

"We didn't order anything. My husband is in Kuwait—he would have told me. There must be a mistake."

The pen in her raised hand was like a funny hostile weapon, and seeing me smile at it, she lowered her hand.

"It's not an order. It's a present. In the van," I said. She looked unbelieving at the van and then back at me. In the awkward pause my mind gave an unintended leap. I forgot about Duggie.

"For you," I said. I seemed to sail away, off my feet.

"For me?" she said. "Why for me?"

I was astonished. Her face went as white as paper and I thought she was going to faint. She stood there, trembling. The pen dropped out of her hand to the floor and she turned around and bent to pick it up and stood up again with a flustered blush as if she had been caught doing something wrong.

"You're the gardener," I said. "Come and look."

She did not move, so I started off down the few steps to the gate. She followed me and I saw her glance, as if calling for protection to the houses on either side of her own.

"Why should you do this?" she said in an unnatural voice. I opened the gate, but she made me go through first.

The swollen rusty pink and skin-white buds of the plant were as bright as candles in the darkness of the van.

"Advertising," I said with a salesman's laugh. She frowned, reproaching me doubtfully. But when she saw the plant she said, "How lovely!"

My tongue raced. I said I had been thinking of the paved circle in the middle of the garden; the magnolia would stand there and flower before the trees shaded the place, and that it could be moved out of the tub wherever she wanted it in the garden later in the year.

"You mean that?" she said.

So I got out a trolley, put up a board and wheeled the plant down from the van carefully. It was very heavy.

"Be careful," she said. She opened the side entrance to the garden and followed me there.

"No muddy puddle now. It's gone," I boasted. It was a struggle getting the heavy tub in place and she helped me.

"You've got a gardener's strong hands," I said.

I looked around and then up at the trees. Her wide mouth opened with delight at the plant.

"How kind you are," she said. "Duggie will love it."

I had never been alone with her in this garden and, I remember, this was privileged ground. She walked around and around the plant as if she were dancing.

"It will be in full bloom in ten days," I said. "It will cheer up the fig tree. It's trying to bud."

"This time of the year," she said, despising it, "that tree looks like a chunk of machinery."

A half-hour passed. We went back to the house and she thanked me again as I pushed the trolley.

"Leave it there," she said. "I must give you some tea or a drink. How lucky I was in. You should have telephoned."

In the sitting room she laughed as she looked back at the plant from the window. It was, I realized, the first time I had heard her laugh. It was surprising not to hear Duggie's voice. She went off to make tea and I sat in an armchair and remembered not to put my dirty hands on the arms. Then I saw my footmarks coming across the carpet to me. I felt I had started on a journey.

I noticed she frowned at them and the cups skidded on the tray when she came back with the tea.

I said apologetically, "My boots!"

Strange words, now that I think of it, for the beginning of a love affair; even she gaped at them as if they had given me away.

When she had only half filled my cup she banged the teapot down, got up and came across to squeeze my hand.

"Oh, you are so *kind, kind,*" she said and then stepped back to her chair quickly.

"You *are* a friend," she said.

And then I saw tears were dropping down her cheeks. Her happy face had collapsed and was ugly. "I'm sorry to be so silly, Mr. Ormerod," she said, trying to laugh.

Ten shelves of Duggie's books looked down, their titles dumb, but listening with all ears as I sat not knowing what to do, for trying to laugh, she sobbed even more and she had to get up and turn her back to me and look out of the window.

"It's all right," she said with her back to me. "Don't let your tea get cold. My husband wanted to put an urn there," she said. "I suppose he told you."

Duggie had not been able to control his drifting mind.

"This is the first time I've been in the garden since you were here last," she said, turning around.

"By the way," I said, "if you're worrying about the shelter, I can tell you—I've looked up the records at the Town Hall. There were no casualties here. There was no one in the shelter."

I did not tell her no records could be traced. Her tears had made. my mind leap again.

"Why on earth did you do that?" she said and she sat down again.

"I had the idea it was worrying you," I said.

"No, not at all," she said, shaking after her cry, and she put on an offhand manner and did not look at me.

"The shelter? Oh, that didn't worry me," she said. "The war was thirty years ago, wasn't it? One doesn't have to wait for bombs to kill people. They die in hospital, don't they? Things prey on my husband's mind. He's a very emotional man; you mightn't think it. I don't know whether he told you, we had trouble with a young man, a tenant. It made Duggie quite ill. They flew him home from Kuwait."

I was baffled. She had exactly reversed the story Duggie had told me.

She said with the firm complacency of a married woman, "He talks himself into things, you know."

After she said this there was a question in her eyes, a movement like a small signal, daring me for a moment. I was silent and she began talking about everyday things, in a nervous way, and intimacy vanished.

She stood at the door and gave a half wave as I left, a scarcely visible wave, like a beckon. It destroyed me. Damn that stupid man, I thought when I got home and stood at the stove getting a meal together. The telephone rang and I turned the stove off. I thought the call was from my mother—it was her hour—but the voice was Sally's, firm but apologetic. "You've left your trolley. I thought you might need it."

O blessed trolley! I said I'd come at once. She said curtly she was going out. That, and the hope that she was not interrupting my dinner, were the only coherent, complete sentences she spoke in one of the longest calls I have ever had. On her side it was a collection of unfinished phrases with long silences between them, so that once or twice she seemed to have gone away—silences in which she appeared to be wrestling with nouns, pronouns and verbs that circled around an apology and explanation that was no explanation, about making "that silly scene." No sooner was she at the point of explanation than she drifted off it. It struck me that listening to her husband so much, she had lost the power of talking.

There was something which, "sometime in the future," she would like to ask me, but it had gone from her mind. "If there is a future," she added too brightly. Her silences dangled and stirred me. The manner was so like Duggie's: it half exasperated me and I asked her if she would have dinner with me one day. "Dinner?" This puzzled her. She asked if I had had my dinner. The idea died and so did the conversation. What affectation, I thought afterwards. Not on my side: desire had been born.

But on the following day I saw her waiting in one of our greenhouses. She was warmer under glass. I had collected my trolley. That, for some reason, pleased her. She agreed to have dinner with me.

"Where on earth are we going?" she said when we drove off.

"Away from the Nursery," I said. I was determined to amuse her. "To get away from the thieves."

"What thieves?" she said.

"The old ladies," I said.

It is well known, if you run a nursery, that very nice old ladies sometimes nip off a stem for a cutting or slip small plants into their bags. Stealing a little is a form of flirtation with them. I said that only this week one of them had come to me when I was alone in a greenhouse and said, "Can I whisper something to you? I have a *dreadful* confession to make. I have been very naughty. I *stole* a snippet of geranium from you in the summer and it has struck!"

Sally said, "And what about old men? Don't they steal?"

My fancy took a leap. "Yes, we've got one," I said, "but he goes in for big stuff."

There was a myth at our Nursery that when a box of plants was missing or some rare expensive shrub had been dug up and was gone, this was the work of a not altogether imaginary person called Thompson who lived in a big house where the garden abutted on our wall. Three camellias went one day, and because of the price he was somehow promoted by the girls and became known as "Colonel" Thompson. He had been seen standing on a stepladder and looking over our wall. I invented a face for the Colonel when I told

Sally about this. I gave him a ripe nose, a bald head, a drooping moustache; unconsciously I was describing Duggie. I went further: I had caught "the Colonel" with one leg over the wall, and when I challenged him he said, "Looking for my dog. Have you seen my dog?"

Sally said, "I don't believe you."

This was promising. A deep seriousness settled on us when we got to the restaurant. It was a small place. People were talking loudly, so that bits of their lives seemed to be flying around us and we soon noticed we were the quietest talkers there, talking about ourselves, but to our plates or the tablecloth, crumbling bread and then looking up with sudden questions. She ate very fast; a hungry woman, I thought. How long, she asked suddenly, raising a fork to her mouth, how long had I known my wife before we were married? Four months, I said. She put her fork down.

"That was a rush," she said. "It took Duggie and me seven years."

"Why was that?"

"I didn't want to get married, of course," she said.

"You mean you lived together?" I said.

"Indeed not. We might not even have married _then,_" she said, "but his firm was sending him to Mexico for three years. We knew each other very well, you know. Actually," she mumbled now, "I was in love with someone else." She now spoke up boldly, "Gratitude is more important than love, isn't it?"

"Is that the question you wanted to ask me," I said, "when you telephoned?"

"I don't think I said that," she said.

I was falling in love with her. I listened but hardly heard what she said. I was listening only to my desire.

"Gratitude? No, I don't," I said. "Not when one is young. Why don't you go with him on his jobs?"

"He likes travel, I don't," she said. "We like each other. I don't mind being alone. I prefer it. You're alone, aren't you?"

Our conversation stopped. A leaden boredom settled on us like a stifling thundercloud. I whispered, looking around first to be sure no one heard me, and in a voice I scarcely recognized as my own, "I want you."

"I know," she said. "It's no good," she said, fidgeting in her chair
and looking down at the cloth. Her movement encouraged me.

"I've loved you ever since—"

She looked up.

"—since you started coming to the Nursery," I said.

"Thank you, but I can't," she said. "I don't go to bed with people.
I gave that up when my daughter was born."

"It's Duggie?" I said.

She was startled and I saw the grimace I knew.

She thought a long time.

"Can't you guess?" she said. And then she leaned across and
touched my hand. "Don't look so gloomy. It's no good with me."

I was not gloomy. That half wave of the hand, the boredom, the
monotony of our voices, even the fact that the people at the next
table had found us so interesting that they too had started whispering, made me certain of how our evening would end.

"Let us go," I said.

I called a waiter and she watched me pay the bill and said, "What
an enormous tip." In our heavy state, this practical remark lightened
us. And for me it had possessive overtones that were encouraging;
she stood outside, waiting for me to bring the car with that air
women have of pretending not to be there. We drove off and when
I turned into a shopping street almost empty at this hour I saw our
heads and shoulders reflected in the windows of a big shop, mocking
us as we glided by: two other people. I turned into a street of villas;
we were alone again and I leaned to kiss her on the neck. She did
not move, but presently she glanced at me and said, "Are you a
friend?"

"No," I said. "I'm not."

"I think I ought to like that," she said. And she gripped my arm
violently and did not let it go.

"Not at my house," she said.

We got to my flat and there she walked across the sitting room
straight to the window and looked down at the long greenhouses
gleaming in the dark.

"Which is Colonel Thompson's house?" she said.

I came up behind her and put my arms around her and she

watched my daring hands play on her breasts with that curiosity and love of themselves that women have, but there was a look of horror on her face when I kissed her on the mouth, a hate that came (I know now) over the years of her marriage. In the next hours it ebbed away, her face emptied and her wide lips parted with greed.

"I don't do things like this," she said.

The next day she came to me; on the third day she pulled me back as I was getting out of bed and said, "Duggie's coming home. I have something bad to tell you, something shameful." She spoke into my shoulder. "Something I tried to tell you when I telephoned, the day you came with the plant, but I couldn't. Do you remember I telephoned to you?

"I told a lie to Duggie about that young man, I told Duggie he attacked me." She said, "It wasn't true. I saw him and his girl at night from my bedroom window going into the garden with their arms round each other, to the end of it, under the trees. They were there a long time. I imagined what they were doing. I could have killed that girl. I was mad with jealousy—I think I was really mad. I went out into the garden many nights to stop them, and in the afternoons I worked there to provoke him and even peeped into their window. It was terrible. So I told Duggie. I told him the boy had come up behind me and pulled at my clothes and tried to rape me. I tore my blouse to prove it. I sent a cable to Duggie. Poor Duggie, he believed me. He came back. I made Duggie throw the boy out. You know what happened. When the boy was killed I thought I would go out of my mind."

"I thought you said Duggie was ill," I said.

"That is what I'm ashamed of," she said. "But I was mad. You know, I hated you too when Duggie brought you in to do those stones. I really hated anyone being in the garden. That is why I made that scene when you brought the magnolia. When you came to the door I thought for an awful moment it was the boy's father coming for his things; he did come once."

I was less shocked than unnerved. I said, "The real trouble was that you were lying to yourself." I saw myself as the rescuer for a moment.

"Do you think he believed you?" I said.

She put on the distant look she used to have when I first met her, almost a look of polite annoyance at being distracted from her story. Then she said something that was true. "Duggie doesn't allow himself to believe what he doesn't want to believe. He never believes what he sees. One day I found him in the sitting room, and he started to pull a book out of the bookcase and closed it with a bang and wiped his eyes. 'Dust,' he said. 'Bad as Mexico.' Afterwards I thought, He's been crying."

"That was because he knew he was to blame," I said.

I went to my window and looked at the sky. In the night he would be coming across it.

"What are we going to do?" I said. "When shall I see you? Are you going to tell him?"

She was very surprised. "Of course not," she said, getting out of bed.

"But we must. If you don't, I shall."

She picked up her dress and half covered herself with it. "If you do," she said. "I'll never see you again, Colonel Thompson."

"He'll find out. I want to marry you."

"I've got a daughter. You forget that. He's my husband."

"He's probably got some girl," I said lightly.

The gentleness went out of our conversation.

"You're not to say that," she said vehemently. We were on the edge of a quarrel.

"I have got to go," she said. "Judy's coming home. I've got to get his suits from the cleaners and there is one of yours."

My suits and Duggie's hanging up on nasty little wire hangers at the cleaners!

We had a crowd of customers at the Nursery and that took my mind off our parting, but when I got back to my flat the air was still and soundless. I walked around my three rooms expecting to see her, but the one or two pictures stared out of my past life. I washed up our empty glasses. Well, there it is, I thought cynically. All over. What do you expect? And I remembered someone saying, "Have an affair with a married woman if you like, but for God's sake don't start wanting to marry her."

It was a help that my secretary was on holiday and I had to do

all the paperwork at night. I also had my contract for replanting the
square the Council had neglected and did a lot of the digging myself.
As I dug I doubted Sally and went over what I knew about her life.
How did she and Duggie meet? What did they say? Was Sally
flaunting herself before her husband, surprising and enticing him?
I was burned by jealousy. Then, at the end of the week, before I left
for the square at half past eight, I heard her steps on the stairs to
my office. She had a busy smile on her face.

"I've brought your suits," she said. "I'm in a rush." And she went
to hang them in their plastic covers on the door, but I had her in
my arms and the suits fell to the floor.

"Is it all right?" I said.

"How do you mean?" she said.

"Duggie," I said.

"Of course," she said complacently.

I locked the door. In a few minutes her doubts and mine were
gone. Our quarrel was over. She looked at me with surprise as she
straightened her skirt.

Happiness! I took one of our girls with me to the square and stood
by lazily watching her get on with her work.

After lunch I was back at the Nursery and I was alarmed to see
Duggie's bald head among the climbing greenery of our hothouse.
He was stooping there, striped by sunlight, like some affable tiger.
I hoped to slip by unseen, but he heard me and the tiger skin
dropped off as he came out, all normality, calling out, "Just the man!
I've been away."

I gave what must have been the first of the small coughs, the first
of a long series with which I would always greet him and which made
him put concern into his voice. I came to call it my "perennial
hybrid"—a phrase that struck him and which he added to his vocab-
ulary of phrases and even to his reflections on coughs in general, on
Arab spitting and Mexican hawking.

"I came over to thank you for that wonderful magnolia. That was
very kind. I missed it in flower but Sally says it was wonderful. You
don't know what it did for her. I don't know whether you have
noticed, she's completely changed. She looks years younger. All her
energy has come back." Then in a louder voice: "She has forgotten

all that trouble. You must have seen it. She tells me she has been
giving you a hand, your girl's away."

"She was very kind. She took my suits to the cleaners."

He ignored this. We walked together across the Nursery and he
waved his hand to the flower beds. Did I say that his daughter was
with him? She was then a fat girl of thirteen or fourteen with fair
hair like her mother's

"Fetched them," said the pedantic child and from that time her
gaze was like a judgment. I picked a flower for her as they followed
me to the door of my office.

"By the way," he said, "what did you do about that fellow who
gets over the wall? Sally told me. Which wall was it?"

Sally seemed to tell him everything.

"He's stopped. That one over there."

He stood still and considered it. "What you need is a wire
fence, with a three-inch mesh to it; if it was wider, the fellow
could get his toe in. It would be worth the outlay—no need to go
in for one of those spiked steel fences we put up round our refiner-
ies." He went on to the general question of fences: he had always
been against people who put broken glass on walls. "Unfair," he
said. He looked lofty— "Cruel, too. Chap who did that ought to
be sent off the field.

"Come and have a drink with us this evening," Duggie said.

I could think of no excuse; in fact, I felt confident and bold now,
but the first person I saw at the house was Duggie wearing a jacket
far too small for him. It was my jacket. She had left his suits at my
office and taken mine to her own house.

Duggie laughed loudly. "Very fishy, I thought, when I saw this
on my bed. Ha! Ha! What's going on? It would be funnier still if
you'd worn mine."

Sally said demurely she saw nothing funny in that. She had only
been trying to help.

"Be careful when Sally tries to help." He was still laughing. The
comedy was a bond. And we kept going back to it. Judy, her daughter, enjoyed this so much that she called out, "Why doesn't Mr.
Ormerod take our flat?"

Our laughter stopped. Children recklessly bring up past inci-

dents in their parents' lives. Duggie was about to pour wine into
Sally's glass and he stopped, holding the bottle in the air. Sally
gave that passing grimace of hers and Duggie shrank into instant
protective concern and to me he seemed to beg us all for silence.
But he recovered quickly and laughed again, noisily—too noisily,
I thought.

"He has to live near the Nursery, don't you, Teddy? Colonel
Thompson and all that."

"Of course," said Sally easily. "Duggie, don't pour the wine on
the carpet, please."

It was a pleasant evening. We moved to the sitting room and Sally
sat on the sofa with the child, who gazed and gazed at me. Sally put
her arm around her.

Three years have passed since that evening when Judy spoke out.
When I look back, those years seem to be veiled or to sparkle with
the mists of an October day. How can one describe happiness? In
due time Duggie would leave and once more for months on end Sally
and I would be free, and despite our bickerings and jealousies, our
arguments about whether Duggie knew or did not know, we fell into
a routine and made our rules. The stamp of passion was on us, yet
there was always in my mind the picture of her sitting on the sofa
with her daughter. I came to swear I would do nothing that would
trouble her. And she and I seemed able to forget our bodies when
we were all together. Perhaps that first comedy had saved us. My
notion was that Duggie invented me, as he had invented her. I spend
my time, she says, inventing Duggie. She invented neither of us.

Now I have changed my mind. After that evening when the child
Judy said, "Why doesn't Mr. Ormerod take our flat?," I am convinced that Duggie *knew*—because of his care for Sally, even because he knew more than either of us about Sally and that tenant
of theirs who was so horribly killed on his motorbike. When he
turned us into fictions he perhaps thought the fiction would soon
end. It did not. He became like a weary, indulgent and distant
emperor when he was home.

But those words of Judy's were another matter. For Duggie, Judy
was not a fiction. She was his daughter, absolutely his, he made her.

She was the contradiction of his failure. About her he would not pretend or compromise. I am now sure of this after one or two trivial events that occurred that year. One afternoon the day before he was due home—one of those enameled misleading October days, indeed —Sally was tidying the bedroom at my flat. I was in the sitting room putting the drinks away and I happened to glance down at the Nursery. I saw a young woman there, with fair hair, just like Sally's, shading her eyes from the sun, and waving. For a moment I thought it was Sally who had secretly slipped away to avoid the sad awkwardness of those businesslike partings of ours. Then I saw the woman was a young girl—Judy. I stepped back out of sight. I called Sally and she came with a broom in her hand.

"Don't go near the window like that"—she was not even wearing a bra—"look!"

"It's Judy! What is she up to? How long has she been there?" she said.

"She's watching us," I said. "She knows!"

Sally made that old grimace I now so rarely see.

"The little bitch," she said. "I left her at home with two of her school friends. She can't know I'm here."

"She must do," I said. "She's spying."

Sally said crisply, "Your paranoia is a rotten cover. Do you think I didn't know that girl's got a crush on you, my sweetheart? Try not to be such a cute old man."

"Me? Try?" I said jauntily.

And then, in the practical manner of one secure in the higher air of unruffled love, she said, "Anyway, she can't see my car from there. She can't see through walls. Don't stand there looking at her."

She went back to tidying the flat and my mind drifted into remembering a time when I was a boy throwing pebbles at the window of the girl next door. What a row there was with her mother!

I forgot Judy's waving arm. Duggie came home and I was not surprised to see him wandering about the Nursery two days later like a dog on one of his favorite rounds, circling around me from a distance, for I was busy with a customer, waiting for his chance. He had brought Judy with him. She was solemnly studying the girls who, with their order books and pencils, were following undecided cus-

tomers or directing the lost to our self-service counter inside the
building. Judy was murmuring to herself as if imagining the words
they said. She was admiring the way one of the girls ordered a youth
to wheel a trolleyload of chrysanthemums to the main gate.

When I was free Duggie came quickly to me. "That counter
works well," he said. He was congratulating himself, for the counter
had been his idea, one item in his dreamy possession of the place.
"It has cut down the labor costs. I've been counting. You've got rid
of three girls, haven't you?"

"Four," I said. "My secretary left last week to get married."

Judy had stopped watching and came up with him. Yes, she had
grown. The child whose face had looked as lumpish as a coffee mug,
colorless too, had suddenly got a figure, and her face was rounded.
Her eyes were moist with the new light of youth, mingling charm-
ingly with an attempt at the look of important experience. She gazed
at me until Duggie stopped talking and then she said, "I saw you
the day before yesterday"—to show she had started to become an
old hand—"at your window. I waved to you."

"Did you?" I said.

"You weren't in your office," she said.

Cautiously I said, "I didn't see you."

"You were ironing your shirts."

A relief.

"Not me. I never iron my shirts," I said. "You must have seen the
man who lives in the flat below. He's always ironing his shirts, poor
fellow. He usually does it at night."

"On the third floor," the girl said.

"I live on the fourth, dear," I said.

"How awful of me," the girl said.

To save her face Duggie said, "I like to see women scrubbing
clothes on stone—on a riverbank."

"That's not ironing, Daddy," she said.

There was the usual invitation to come to his house for a drink
now that he was back. I did my cough and said I might drop in,
though as he could see, we were in a rush. When I got to his house
I found a chance to tell Sally. "Clever of her," I said. "It was a
scheme to find out which floor I live on."

"It was not what you think," Sally said.

The evening was dull and Sally looked unwell and went to bed early. Duggie and I were left to ourselves and he listened to me in an absent-minded way when I told him again about my secretary leaving. He said, grumpily, "You ought leave the girls alone and go in for older women," and went on to say that his sister-in-law was coming to stay, suggesting that married life also had its troubles. Suddenly he woke up, and as if opportunity had been revealed to him in a massive way he said, "Come and have dinner with me at my club tomorrow."

The invitation was half plea half threat. *He* was being punished. Why not myself also?

Duggie's club! Was this to be a showdown? The club was not a bolt-hole for Duggie. It was an imperial institution in his life and almost sacred. One had to understand that, although rarely mentioned, it was headquarters, the only place in England where he was irrefutably himself and at home with his mysteries. He did not despise me for not having a club myself, but it did explain why I had something of the homeless dog about me. That clubs bored me suggested a moral weakness. I rose slightly in his esteem once when I told him that years ago my uncle used to take me to *his* club. (He used to give me a lot to drink and lecture me on my feckless habits and even introduced me to one or two members—I suppose to put stamina in me.) These invitations came after my wife's death, so that clubs came to seem to me places where marriages were casketed and hidden by the heavy curtains on the high windows.

There was something formidable in Duggie's invitation, and when I got to his club my impression was that he had put on weight or had received a quiet authority from being only among men, among husbands, in mufti. It was a place where the shabby armchairs seemed made of assumptions in leather and questions long ago disposed of. In this natural home Duggie was no longer inventive or garrulous. Nods and grunts to the members showed that he was on his true ground.

We dined at a private table. Duggie sat with his back to an old brocade curtain in which I saw some vegetable design that perhaps had allayed or taken over the fantasies of the members.

A couple of drinks in the bar downstairs and a decanter of wine on the table eased Duggie, who said the old chef had had a stroke and that he thought the new chef had not got his hand in yet. The sweetbreads had been runny the last time; maybe it would be better to risk the beef.

Then he became confessional to put me at my ease: he always came here when his sister-in-law came to stay. A difficult woman— he always said to Sally, "Can't you put her off? You'll only get one of your migraines after she has been."

"I thought Sally didn't look too well," I said.

"She's having a worrying time with Judy," he said. "Young girls grow up. She's going through a phase."

"She is very lovely."

He ignored this. "Freedom, you know! Wants to leave school. Doesn't work. Messed up her exams."

"Sex, I suppose," I said.

"Why does everyone talk about sex?" said Duggie, looking stormy. "She wants to get away, get a flat of her own, get a job, earn her living, sick of the old folks. But a flat of her own—at sixteen! I ask you."

"Girls have changed."

Duggie studied me and made a decision. I now understood why I had been asked.

"I wondered," said Duggie, "has she ever said anything to you— parents are the last to hear anything."

"To me?"

"Friend of the family—I just wondered."

"I hardly ever see her. Only when Sally or you bring her to the Nursery. I can't see the young confiding in me. Not a word."

Duggie was disappointed. He found it hard to lose one of his favorite fancies: that among all those girls at the Nursery I had sublimated the spent desires of my youth. He said, taking an injured pride in a fate, "That's it. I married into a family of gardeners."

And then he came out with it—the purpose of this dinner: "The girl's mad to get a job in your nursery. I thought she might have been sounding you out—I mean, waving to that fellow ironing his shirt."

"No. Nothing," I said.

"Mad idea. You're turning people away! I told her. By the way, I don't want to embarrass you. I'm not suggesting you should take her on. Girls get these ideas. Actually, we're going to take her away from that school and send her to school in Switzerland. Alps, skiing. Her French and German are a mess. Abroad! That is what she needs."

Abroad! The most responsive string in Duggie's nature had been struck. He meant what he said.

"That will be hard on Sally," I said. "She'd miss her terribly."

"We've got to do the best for the girl. She knows that," said Duggie.

And without warning the old stare, but now it was the stare of the interrogator's lamp, turned on my face, and his manner changed from the brisk and businesslike to the commandingly offhand.

"Ironical," he said. "Now, if Sally had wanted a job at your nursery, that would be understandable. After all, you deal with all those Dutch and French, and so on. Her German's perfect. But poor Judy, she can't utter."

"Sally!" I laughed. "She'd hate it."

Duggie filled my glass and then his own very slowly, but as he raised the decanter he kept his eye on me: quite a small feat, indeed like a minor conjuring trick, for a man who more than once had knocked a glass over at home and made Sally rush to the kitchen for a cloth.

"You're quite wrong," he said. "I happen to know."

Know what? "You mean *she's* mentioned it," I said.

"No, no, of course not," he said. "But if you said the word, I'm certain of it. Not last year perhaps. But if Judy goes to Switzerland, she'll be alone. She'd jump at it."

Now the wine began to work on him—and on me, too—and Duggie's conversation lost its crisp manner. He moved on to one of his trailing geographical trances; we moved through time and space. The club became subtropical, giant ferns burst out of the club curtains, liana hung from the white pillars of the dining room, the other members seemed to be in native dress, and threading through it all was the figure of Sally, notebook in hand. She followed us downstairs to the bar, which became a greenhouse, as we drank our port. No longer wretched because her daughter had gone, no longer fretting about the disastrous mess she had made of her life when she was young, without a mother's experience to guide her. I heard Duggie say, "I know they're moving me to Brussels in a few months and of course I'll be over every weekend—but a woman wants her own life. Frankly," he said with awe in his voice, "we *bore* them."

The club resumed its usual appearance, though with an air of exhaustion. The leather chairs yawned. The carpets died. A lost member rose from the grave and stopped by Duggie and said, "We need a fourth at bridge."

"Sorry, old boy," said Duggie.

The man went off to die elsewhere.

"And no danger," said Duggie, "of her leaving to get married."

And now, drunkish as we were, we brought our momentous peace conference to an end. The interrogator's lamp was switched on again just before we got to our feet and he seemed to be boring his way into my head and to say, "You've taken my wife, but you're bloody well not going to get my daughter into your pokey little fourth-floor flat ironing your shirts."

I saw the passion in his mottled face and the powerful gleam of his honorable head.

After Sally had put up a fight and I had said that sending Judy away was his revenge, Sally came to work for me. Duggie had married us and I became as nervous and obsequious as a groom. There was the awkwardness of a honeymoon. She dressed differently. She became sedate—no strokings and squeezes of love were allowed: she frowned and twisted away like a woman who had been a secretary all her life. She looked as young and cross as a virgin. She went back to her straight-back hair style; I was back in the period when I was disturbed by the soft hair of her eyebrows. Her voice was all telephone calls, invoices, orders and snapping at things I had forgotten to do. She walked in a stately way to the filing cabinet. Only to that object did she bend: she said what a mess her predecessor or I had left it in. If she went downstairs to the yard when the lorries arrived, she had papers in her hand. The drivers were cocky at first and then were scared of her. And in time she destroyed our legend—the only unpopular thing she did—the legend of Colonel Thompson. Dog or no dog, he had never come over the wall. The thief, she discovered, had been one of our gardeners. So Colonel Thompson retired to our private life.

Before this, our life had been one of beginnings, sudden partings, unexpected renewals. Now it hummed plainly along from day to day. The roles of Duggie and myself were reversed: when Duggie came home once a week now from Brussels it was he who seemed to be the lover and I the husband. Sally grew very sharp with both of us and Duggie and I stood apart, on our dignity.

I have done one thing for him. I took my mother to dine with him, as I have said.

"What a saintly man," she said as we drove away. "Just like your father. He's coming to see me next time they're at their cottage."

V. S. PRITCHETT was born in 1900. In addition to being a short-story writer, he is a critic, autobiographer, biographer, novelist and travel writer. Sir Victor is a foreign honorary member of the American Academy of Arts and Letters and of the Academy of Arts and Sciences. In 1975 he received a knighthood. He lives in London with his wife.